TRIXIE'S TREATS, VOL. II

TRIXIE'S TREATS, VOL. II

A ghostly haunting, an office romance, a rescue on turbulent waters, an irresistible bet, a house of dreams, and an intimate party add incredible spice to a wonderful buffet of tasty heroes from erotic romance author Trixie Stilletto.

Previously available only in electronic format, these steamy stories of erotic romance have now been combined—due to popular demand—for a paperback edition!

Included are the tales...

The Business Trip
Molding Clay
The Coming
Framed In Dreams
Hero Adrift
Party for Two

"4 Blue Ribbon Rating!...*The Business Trip* is hot enough to melt the winter snow in Alaska."

—Dina Smith, *Romance Junkies*

"Trixie Stilletto has earned herself a rating of 4 Angels for this work of art [*Molding Clay*]."

—Jessica, *Fallen Angel Reviews*

TRIXIE'S TREATS, VOL. II

BY

TRIXIE STILLETTO

AMBER QUILL PRESS, LLC
http://www.amberquill.com

TRIXIE'S TREATS, VOL. II
AN AMBER QUILL PRESS BOOK

Amber Quill Press, LLC
http://www.amberquill.com

Layout and Formatting provided by: ElementalAlchemy.com

PUBLISHED IN THE UNITED STATES OF AMERICA

To Trace for helping me keep the faith!

TABLE OF CONTENTS

THE BUSINESS TRIP

CHAPTER 1

His hand trailed up her ivory, stocking-covered leg until his fingers touched the edge of her skin. He toyed lightly with the garter holding the stockings up, running his fingers across the lace and stroking the quivering skin of her thigh.

"My dear, you are so very responsive," he murmured. His fingers moved higher and she held....

Shit, the boss is coming. Close file. Close file.

"Ms. Montgomery, were you able to schedule a pick up for this afternoon to get the documents to China?"

Eliza Montgomery pushed her glasses back up her nose and hoped to goodness her boss, Clayton Johnson, couldn't tell she was sweating like a virgin on her wedding night.

"Uhmm, yes sir. They should be here at three. They're charging extra to come on the holiday, though."

"Can't be helped." Johnson moved a little closer to her desk. She felt her nervous tension change to a different kind of tension—one that caused the muscles and nerves deep inside her abdomen, and lower, to wake up. That always seemed to happen around Clayton Johnson. She wished just once he'd look at her with some thing more than professional inquiry in his eyes.

"Are you all right, Ms. Montgomery? You look a little flushed."

If only you knew, she thought. Aloud she said, "Yes, sir. I mean, no, sir."

Johnson scowled. It was a shame. That seemed to be his perpetual look when he dealt with her. Eliza almost sighed. He was such a handsome man. Check that, actually Clayton Johnson was a hunk. A drop-your-tongue, loose-the-ability-to-think-rationally, hunka-hunka burning man. He was six-foot four inches of solid muscle. His coal black hair, with just a touch of silver at the temples, made a girl long to run her hands through it. And what he did for those Brooks Brothers suits he favored.... Well, that was another sin. He had eyes so dark a blue that sometimes she felt like she could willingly drown in them.

For a girl growing up playing with Barbie and Ken dolls, and dreaming a man who looked and acted like Tom Selleck would come and take her away, Clayton Johnson was every dream come true.

It was just a shame he never smiled. At least not at the office. Maybe one of his fabulous escorts made him smile. Liza kind of doubted it, though. It seemed to her, since he left the entire calling and setting of the dates to her, that he attacked the dating scene with the same humorless approach he attached to his work. Yes, Clayton Johnson had to be the original poster boy for the all-work-no-play campaign.

Come to think of it, she mused, *I haven't either arranged one of his dates or taken any messages from his women in several months.* Maybe that was part of the reason he was such a grouch lately. He needed to get laid. She almost smiled at the thought of what his reaction would be should she offer her own body for the good of the employees so to speak.

"Which is it, Ms. Montgomery?" he growled.

Liza gulped again. "I'm fine, sir."

"Good. There's been some kind of virus hitting the company. We had three people call in sick in receiving this morning."

Gee, wonder why? Liza thought uncharitably. *It is after all, New Year's Day. Most people were busy being hung over after ringing in the New Year. And most companies don't bother opening on a national holiday.*

Then again Johnson Electronics wasn't most companies. They were open every day except Sunday year around. Granted, he paid double time on the holidays, but Clayton Johnson could never seem to quite understand that some things were more important than money.

Liza almost sighed. She wished there were more important things than money in her life. But a girl had to eat and pay bills in today's world. Unless, of course, you were lucky enough to live in the pages of a novel. Liza wasn't that fortunate. But she could dream. In those dreams, Liza was the type of woman who could make Clayton Johnson stand up on his tiptoes and beg for mercy.

At the sound of his throat clearing, Liza jolted back to reality. She wasn't that kind of woman. She had to admit it. She was an executive assistant, not a member of the rich and famous club. She was a little too heavy for her own liking and forced to wear boxy business suits, which made her already generous bosom look like it could launch a fleet of carriers. She also had a few pants outfits with long over blouses that looked good in the catalogue, but failed miserably on short women with hips that rivaled the width of the Grand Canyon.

But, it never hurt to dream, right?

So every day she worked alongside Scrooge, er, Clayton Johnson, Liza wished she was someone else.

That thought made her grin. She needed to be more like Satin Pleasure, queen of erotic romance. Oh, wouldn't that be a sight to send Clayton's neat, little world into a wild tailspin?

"Ms. Montgomery?"

Liza shook her head and realized Johnson was staring at her as if she had grown another eye. "I'm sorry. Did you want something else?"

"Yes, Ms. Montgomery, I did. If you truly feel well today, please bring your keypad and come into my office. I have some memos I want to dictate."

He turned and strode into his office. Liza had the irrational urge to imitate his walk while sitting at her desk and sticking out her tongue at him. Of course, Liza wouldn't dare do that. Now, Satin would. Heck, Satin would have followed Clayton Johnson and offered to do something wild like spreading peanut butter all over his delectable body and licking it off. The picture that popped into Liza's head at that thought was highly erotic. *Yum. Peanut butter. With just a smidgen of jelly. Grape,* she decided. *Nah, he'd never go for that. But how about hot fudge?*

Satin had written about the amazing uses for hot fudge in her last story, "Afternoon Delights." That was the one which had won the coveted Passion Prose award from a famous magazine. It had also been nominated for the prestigious Seraphina award from the Erotic Romance Writers Association.

The words Satin had used popped immediately into Liza's mind.

The man was naked except for the dollop of hot fudge covering the tip of his erect cock.

"Oooh, there's nothing better than a sundae," the woman purred.

"I agree," the corporate pirate said. *"As long as you're the cherry on top."*

"Oh, I think you'll find my cherry just to your liking," the woman said before kneeling in front of him and wrapping her mouth around him.

Liza immediately got a picture of Clayton wearing nothing but his tie and a generous dollop of hot fudge. She sighed. There was no chance it would ever happen. He saw her as his efficient and slightly dumpy employee. That's all.

Eliza straightened her spine and reached in the drawer for her keypad. She had to stop thinking about herself like that. So, she wasn't a size five. She actually had cleavage and curves. She had to start thinking like Satin would.

Satin would not think of herself as dumpy. Satin was full-figured. Satin was a Rubenesque babe that real men could hold on to. That was how Liza would think of herself from now on. It was her New Year's resolution. She was going to grab all the gusto in life she could.

Feeling her spine straighten and her shoulders pull back with resolve, Liza grabbed up her keyboard and headed into Clayton's office.

Memos. How silly was that? He runs an electronics firm, she thought. Yet he can't even type his own memos.

Not that she minded getting all the latest gadgets like this nifty little keyboard.

It worked like a laptop but weighed only half a pound and came with infrared technology so she could send all her typing directly into their mainframe. It also had a recorder with voice recognition software so she hardly had to type. This same technology was why it was so silly Johnson refused to do his own memos and letters.

And sometimes gadgets just weren't enough to keep a girl happy. At least not this type of gadget. There had been a gadget Satin once wrote about in "Toys for Her," one of Liza's personal favorite short stories. Nothing as pedestrian as a plain, ordinary dildo, the one the heroine of that story used felt like skin and had a small heater in it to simulate warm flesh as it got erect. Of course, Satin hadn't made her heroine suffer with electronic stimulation alone. Satin always gave her heroines a nice hunky man to play with in the end.

In "Toys for Her," the couple had played a very dexterous form of the game Twister, achieving mind-blowing orgasms.

Liza sighed and thought again that she should have called in sick today like her roommate. Maybe she would have, if she'd had some of the gadgets Satin had written about in "Toys for Her." Or better yet, one of Satin's heroes. Just thinking about them made Liza squirm a little. The best guy was Cale in "Pirates of Pantzance." He'd been too yummy for words when the heroine had been ravaged by him on a deserted island. It made her want to escape to her own tropical island, but of course, only if she could take Cale with her.

Just because she hadn't had sex in more than three years didn't mean she had no sex drive. It just meant that it had been a long dry spell.

Well, dry spell or not, Liza had work to do, and Clayton Johnson was not a patient man. One thing she couldn't handle was another afternoon of Clayton sulking.

Clayton swiveled from his view of downtown Buffalo when she walked into his office. Today's lake effect snowstorm had already come and gone leaving in its wake a winter wonderland, pure white and glittering throughout the city. The sun, bouncing off the snow and the gleaming buildings surrounding them, momentarily blinded Liza. For a second, it appeared as if her boss had a halo. She shook her head and all angelic references fled. He was simply so handsome he took her breath away.

"About time, Ms. Montgomery. I thought for a moment you'd forgotten about me."

Liza nearly sighed again. Did she mention that her boss was impatient? She settled into the chair facing his desk, crossed her legs at the ankles demurely, turned on the machine and waited.

When he didn't say anything for a moment, she glanced up. His eyes were latched on to her legs. Right. That might happen.

Good Lord, she really needed to do something about her libido if she actually thought Clayton Johnson was looking at her body.

Oh, shucks, maybe I have a run, she thought immediately. *And I just bought this pair last week.*

She twisted a little, trying to see where the run was. When she looked up again, she actually thought she saw him blush.

"Is anything wrong, sir?"

"Er, no. Let's get on with it."

Liza bristled. "I've been ready."

"Yes." Mr. Johnson actually ran his finger around his collar.

He is embarrassed, Liza thought. *Finally, a hint of humanity from him.*

"First, I want to let you know there's been a change in the schedule for the rest of this month."

Back to business. She must have imagined the show of emotion. Perhaps he was a robot. Liza knew their R&D department had been working on a model...

"Ms. Montgomery..." The frustrated impatience was back.

"Oh, sorry." Liza dropped the keyboard and pulled her PDA out of her pocket. She had the company schedule open in seconds. "Okay, I'm ready now."

"The Buffalo office will be closed for the last two weeks of January."

Liza nearly dropped her stylus. "Closed? The entire office?"

"That's right. I'm giving everyone an extra two weeks off with pay. In appreciation for the great year we had last year."

"Hallelujah," Liza murmured.

"What's that, Ms. Montgomery?"

"Er, I said that's very generous, sir. I'm sure the employees will be ecstatic!"

"Yes, well, there's more."

Liza eagerly moved forward in her seat. Already she was planning her vacation. Maybe she'd take a cruise. It would be tight on her budget so soon after the holidays, but what the heck, a girl didn't often get the chance to get out of a Buffalo winter. And it would be the perfect opportunity to put her new life motto to work. Especially if she could find a cruise to a deserted tropical island. Heck, even an undeserted island would be terrific, and worth every hefty cent she put on her credit card. Bermuda would be great. Or she could go to Puerto Rico.

"We, of course, will be using that time well."

It took a moment for his words to filter through her mind.

"We?" she croaked.

"That's right Ms. Montgomery. I have a business trip to make. Alaska. And I want you to go with me."

"Alaska? A-l-a-s-k-a?"

"That's right. There's a big oil company based there looking to integrate new technology to control their pipelines. I mean for Johnson Electronics to win their contract."

"But why me? Why do I have to go with you?"

"I need you, Ms. Montgomery. There's going to be a lot of information exchanged in meetings. I need my executive assistant with me."

"But what about my extra two weeks? Don't I get any time off?"

"You're salaried. I made it clear from the start that I expect more from my salary people. It's part of the job."

"But—"

"No buts, Ms. Montgomery. We need to get moving on this immediately. We'll need reservations to Anchorage. Then, as I understand it, it'll only be a short two- to three-hour ride up into the Chugach Mountains where the oil company has a retreat. They'll provide transport from Anchorage. We'll be leaving two weeks from today."

Well, damn, Liza thought. *What would Satin do now?*

*   *   *

The dark-haired man's hand moved up the stockings and slowly traced the edge of the garter, kissing the woman senseless in the process. It was a wet, noisy kiss, with their tongues busily mating, lips open wide. She felt like all she wanted was to swallow him whole. His dark blue eyes sparkled with desire and she felt as if she was melting…

Bleep, bleep, bleep, bleep, bleep.

Liza groaned and put the pillow over her head to block out the sound of her alarm clock going crazy.

God, timing.

She had the world's worst timing in the world. It never failed. She was always getting woken up or interrupted before she got to the good parts. She reached out and pressed the off button. She wanted more than ever to roll over and go back to her dream. But Clayton Johnson and Alaska were waiting for her. She wished she had the nerve to tell him to take his job and shove it. She wished, just once, Clayton would look at her the way the man in her dream had.

Liza pushed back the covers. She wasn't going to quit and she wasn't going to complain about going to Alaska. She didn't have what it took. But when she returned, she and Clayton Johnson were going to have it out. No more excuses.

CHAPTER 2

Clay Johnson looked over at his executive secretary as she slept in the chair beside him. They were on the second leg of their journey. It had been nothing like he expected, and he wasn't the least happy.

He wasn't unhappy with her. In fact, Eliza's buoyant sense of humor was the only thing that kept him from going off. To be honest, it wasn't only her buoyant humor that was a steadying force. The fact was his executive assistant was a knockout. It didn't matter what she wore. The business suits that made him want to forget all about work when the little slit at the back showed off those amazing little legs. Or what she was wearing now—the black leggings with thick socks showing at her ankles, the clunky little boots that shouldn't have been sexy, and a wool sweater that made him thank his Maker for cold weather.

Clay remembered veterans of World War II talking about the impact of the poster girls—busty starlets in sweater dresses—on the fighting men. He'd never really gotten it. But this was the first time he'd seen Eliza in the clingy wool material. Now he was thinking a company-wide memo requiring sweaters be worn at least once a week wouldn't be out of line at all.

Yes, this was supposed to be a business trip. At least that's what Liza thought. But he had plans for much more. There was only one problem. Everything that could go wrong had.

Their flight from Buffalo had been delayed due to a snow squall. The small, modern but intimate Cessna scheduled for the last leg that should have been just him and her and the pilot, turned out to be a reject from World War II held together with rubber bands and chicken wire. They were supposed to be sipping perfectly chilled champagne in reserved but richly appointed splendor, where they could cuddle and watch the majestic, raw beauty of Alaska unfold beneath them.

Instead, there was no time for romantic anything. All either one of them could do was hang on for dear life against the unbelievable turbulence and pray for their lives. At least neither had to use the barf bags so thoughtfully provided by their pilot.

The plane hit a particularly deep pocket of dead air and dropped quickly. He looked over at Eliza's green face. He felt the answering swirl in his stomach.

Yet...

Whatever had possessed him to think of wooing this woman with a business trip to Alaska? He should have stuck with Bermuda like his best friend had suggested. But no, he had to try to do things in the roundabout way. He'd thought this would be more romantic. Alone, surrounded by rustic yet well-heeled beauty in southeastern Alaska. Nothing to do but make love in front of a roaring fire, make love snuggled on a deep feather bed, make love anywhere their hearts desired.

It had taken a bit of planning and maneuvering on his part. He'd had to pay a hefty fee to convince the owner they should be the only ones renting the ten-room lodge for this weekend.

And this pilot and plane, which didn't look anything like the picture on the internet website, had cost much more than a weekend jaunt to Bermuda would have.

Well, next time, he promised himself, he would not try subversion. Next time... Good God, he hoped he never again had to trick this woman into joining him, but if there was a next time, he was just going to do something normal.

Trick Eliza Montgomery. That was what this had come down to. He'd been too afraid she'd turn him down, so instead of just taking the chance and asking her out like any other normal woman, he'd chickened out.

He told himself it was because he didn't want her to think she had to go out with him because of her job. He'd wanted to do something worthy of a hero in a romance novel.

Now, instead of just winning over his elusive executive assistant's heart, he had to keep her from throwing up.

*   *   *

Poor Mr. Johnson, Eliza thought as she saw the angry twitching along the strong muscle of his jaw. *He's not a happy camper.*

If she wasn't so busy battling airsickness, she might feel sorry for him. Obviously he'd expected something a little flashier and modern from the company he was hoping to do business with. He had been expecting to be met by the company officials, not some scruffy looking bush pilot who appeared to be lost in the '60s—1860s, that is. The pilot also—she sniffed and wrinkled her nose—either had a severe gland problem or hadn't seen a bar of soap in a month of Sundays. She laughed at the thought.

"Did you say something?" Clayton turned and looked at her as he yelled the question over the sound of the engines.

Eliza looked at him and decided to give the guy a break. After all, this wasn't his fault. "No," she replied. "At least the scenery is special. Look."

He leaned over and looked out the window on her side, his arm brushing hers and his rock hard thigh edging against her leg. Eliza's breath caught at the electric thrill that moved through her. She imagined his strength holding her, molding her, as they brought each other to the edge of ecstasy.

She shook her head at her whimsy. He would not be bringing her to the edge of anything. Not as long as she looked the way she did. He looked like a Greek God. Today, dressed down in jeans that fit him as faithfully as a lover, a cotton flannel shirt that molded his rock hard abs and perfectly developed pecs, shoulders and arms, and rugged work boots, Clayton Johnson looked like a strapping lumberjack, ready to rescue a damsel in distress.

He looked like he would still have the stamina to hammer into said damsel all day and all night. Her eyes lingered on his package, encased in denim but still obvious, and her mouth watered.

She realized he was looking at her oddly and stammered as she felt the blush riding to her cheeks. "I'm sorry...what did you say?"

"I said you're right. The scenery is special. So are you."

Eliza felt a different kind of thrill move through her. She felt her smile widen. "Why thank you, Mr. Johnson. I thought you'd never notice."

"Call me Clay, please. After all, we're in the back of beyond. I think some of the office formality can be lost, don't you?"

"Yes," she agreed. "I'm not a big fan of formality."

He smiled. Eliza responded. Mr. Johnson, er, Clay was always handsome, but when that smile of his widened across his sensuous full lips and lit up those wonderful eyes, he was mouthwateringly perfect.

"I've noticed that," he said. He looked like he was about to say more when suddenly the plane banked sharply. The plane skimmed over the top of lush, evergreen trees so dense Liza wondered if any human had seen them from the ground up in decades. Though she knew there was no danger, she caught her breath. The tops looked so close that she could have reached out and touched them.

Then, as if startled by their appearance, a beautiful eagle took flight racing even with their plane before peeling out away from them as if tired of playing with silly humans.

The plane turned again and suddenly the forest dropped away. Below, glistening in the bright sun was a perfect lake. Although there was snow covered ice stretching out from the shoreline, it must have been nearly as deep as at its center as Lake Erie because there the water was such a pure blue Liza could see the darker shapes of fish skimming along under the surface.

As they came down, their water landing gear touching the lake, a huge log cabin came into view at the far end. She caught her breath at the sheer beauty of the picture.

"Oh, look," she exclaimed. "Isn't it wonderful?"

This was just like Satin's story "Alaskan Desire," only much more vivid. There was snow, of course, but it looked even whiter than it did when it glistened on Lake Erie at home. As beautiful as the scenery was, she realized that the man sitting next to her was even more capable of stealing her breath. The hero in "Alaskan Desire" had been a lumberjack with a cock like a saber saw. When she closed her eyes, she saw her boss dressed in work boots and nothing else.

It would take all her control to keep from jumping his bones the minute they landed.

*   *   *

Clay smiled. Finally, things were beginning to be what he expected. He looked around the luxurious cabin as their pilot set their luggage on the floor. There was a great room with gleaming hardwood floors, a long, comfortable sofa, a couple of chairs that looked big enough to easily fit two people in front of a mammoth stone fireplace. There was a fire burning cheerfully and a huge bearskin rug taking up the bulk of the floor space in front of it. His palms itched with the overwhelming desire to see a naked Eliza lounging on the rug in front of the fire.

"Wow," she said, echoing his thoughts. "I can't say much for the trip in, but this place is fantastic."

"Yes," he agreed.

She walked forward into the large room. His gaze lingered on the way her leggings faithfully outlined her stupendous ass. Now, his fingers and his cock itched for another reason.

He reached in his pocket, grabbed a wad of cash without looking and handed it to the pilot. He took the hint and left them alone.

Clayton moved forward following Eliza as she wandered through the first level of the house. It was a little disconcerting because each room they entered put fantasies in his mind of what he would like to do with his assistant.

In the kitchen, as she exclaimed over the state of art commercial stove and work island, he saw himself lifting her on top of said counter. She would gasp in surprise, but would soon warm up to their activities.

Suddenly, something inside him snapped. He'd been fantasying about being with her in a situation like this from the day she'd started to work for him. Now, he couldn't wait any longer. With her back facing him, he walked over and wrapped his arms around her waist pulling her luscious ass full against his cock.

"Mr. Johnson," she screeched.

"For God's sake, call me Clay," he murmured. Incredibly, he felt her butt cheeks flexing. The result created a natural canal that measured him like a leather glove. He lowered his head and nibbled on her neck. It was like tasting ambrosia. He'd been dying to find out if the scent she wore day in and day out at the office was bottled or something else.

As a wave of cinnamon and spice drifted over him, he knew the smell was uniquely Eliza. Over the year-and-a-half she'd worked for him, he'd found himself waking up in the middle of the night with a raging hard-on with that exact smell lingering through his mind.

When she gasped and tilted her neck to give his mouth better access, he took advantage, nibbling his way from her ear lobe down to the tender indentation of her shoulder. At the same time, his hands moved up from her waist and gently stroked the edges of her breasts. Even through her sweater, he could feel the wonderful weight of them. Her hand moved and rubbed through his hair at the crown of his head. He raised his head. He had to give her one chance to stop things before it was too late. If she said no now, he didn't know how he'd handle it, but he knew he had to give her the chance.

"Eliza," he said, turning her so she faced him. "You make the choice."

Her eyes were glorious, luminous with her desire. He felt hope burgeoning along with every thing else south of his border.

"On the rug or in the bed?" she purred.

"Both." He wrapped his arms around her waist and lifted her off the floor. She laughed along with him as their lips met in a hungry kiss that soon turned their sounds to moans.

She was sweet and tangy at the same time as his tongue darted across her lips and entered her mouth to explore the taste and textures he found there. Hot, wet heat met his tongue, along with just a hint of the spearmint gum she had chewed in the airplane to keep her ears from popping.

He finally broke off the kiss long moments later. She leaned her head against his chest and he knew she could feel the racing of his heart. The way her breath was rasping through her lips told him she was just as excited as he. He bent slightly and then put an arm under her legs, picking her up and striding rapidly into the living room. The bedroom would definitely have to wait for round two.

He laid her gently down on the bearskin rug and leaned back on his heels with his hands on his thighs. She smiled at him before removing her sweater. He caught his breath as the flesh of her midriff was slowly revealed to him. It was white and just a bit rounded. He felt himself getting even harder, if possible, at the sight of her luscious body being revealed to him.

That was the only real problem here. Things were not progressing fast enough. He felt the need for speed. Hoping she'd get the hint, he tore off his own clothes and threw them behind him. Finally, he was kneeling in front of her, naked and with his cock standing at full alert. For a second, just a second, he had that flash of insecurity. Would she find him pleasing? Too big? Or God help him, too small?

"God, you're beautiful," she murmured, licking her lips. Her tongue left a light trail of moisture over her ruby red lips and he felt his balls swelling, drawing tightly against his body in arousal, all insecurities forgotten.

Her sweater was now off and his eyes feasted on the bounty of her full breasts. The black lace of her bra was a stark counterpoint to her creamy skin but also hid her nipples from him. He wondered if they would be the same color as her lips or something deeper. He reached forward and gently ran a finger over her, tracing the outline of lace from where it met the bra's strap to the cleavage the cup formed. He dipped his pinky into that crevice and watched as her nostrils flared and her eyes widened in pleasure.

"You're so responsive," he murmured before bending his head to let his lips and tongue follow the journey his fingers had completed.

While his mouth was busy discovering the tastes and textures, his hands weren't idle. With his left, he walked his fingers down her spine, over the waistband of her slacks and down to cup her right butt cheek, squeezing and releasing the soft flesh encased in knit. With his right hand, he dipped underneath the material covering her left breast until he could pluck her turgid nipple. It was hard and he couldn't help but press and pull on it.

"Oh, God, Clay," she moaned. "Please."

"Oh, I intend to. Please us both." He dispatched her bra and took his first complete look at her unbound breasts. He gasped.

They were heavy with thin blue veins just barely visible under her ivory skin, and her large areolas were just a shade darker than her ruby lips. And they were his.

He suckled first the right, drawing the nipple and as much of her breast as he could deep into his mouth. He drew his tongue slowly over her, pressing the nipple against the roof of his mouth to gain the most friction. He could happily stay there for a lifetime, but there was so much more to explore that he knew he needed to move on.

He pulled his mouth from her and ran his finger around the puckered areola, delighting in the moan that escaped her mouth. He switched his attention to the left nipple.

When both tips were wet from his saliva and she was gasping his name and thrusting her breasts eagerly toward him, he pushed her mounds together and took both nipples in his mouth at once.

He felt the orgasm start at the top of her body and roll all the way through her. It was so intense it shook him to the core as well.

Then Clay Johnson did something he hadn't done in decades. He lost complete control and came all over her, his cream soaking her pants.

CHAPTER 3

He was still for a moment then hurriedly pulled away. *What an idiot,* he thought. *I'm acting like a boy experiencing his first throes of passion.* He turned back to apologize to her, but stopped before uttering a word when he saw the smug look on her face.

"Well, cowboy, that was a rocket ride," she said before she stood, and removed her pants and panties.

She was shaved as bare as a baby and he could see the glistening moisture on her pussy lips. He turned onto his knees and moved back toward her. His hands wrapped around her butt and pulled her to him.

"Let me see if I can make things last a little longer this time," he murmured then buried his face in her pussy.

*   *   *

Eliza closed her eyes and held his head against her as she felt his mouth worshipping her. Her breath stuttered out as his nose separated the folds of her labia and his tongue flicked across her slit.

This felt much better than she imagined when reading "Alaskan Desire" was the only thought in her head.

When Clay's tongue flicked once, then twice over her nub before sucking it deeply into his mouth, she felt as if he was pulling her soul right out of her body.

Finally, he pulled his mouth away from her. She could see the evidence of her arousal lingering on his lips. She fell to her knees and cupped his huge testicles in her hands. He had brought her so much pleasure. The least she could do was return the favor. She reached for his nipples.

Moving slowly, her hand traced its way down his chest, following the line of black hair as it arrowed its way past rock-hard abs. She knew he had a membership at one of Buffalo's most exclusive gyms. She could see he had taken advantage of it, and felt a momentary pang at the fact her body would never grace the cover of any fitness magazine.

As she traced a circle around his belly button, she put the last thought from her mind. There was no room for insecurities here. And, as his cock waved his arousal at her, she did what came naturally. She placed her fingers at the base and then licked him from the bottom to the very top with one slow, unending swipe. When she reached the slit, she used the tip of her tongue to delve deeply, tasting the remnants of his last orgasm. It was sweet and tangy with just the right amount of salt. His hand clenched her hair, holding her still against him.

She willingly took the hint and sucked the bulbous head into her mouth, letting her teeth scrape gently against the ridge just under the mushroom top. It was like licking a hot, seductive lollypop. But this was like no lollypop she'd ever had before. This was hot, hard steel wrapped in the most delicious soft coating.

She knew how to give a man oral sex. She'd had done a lot of research on the internet. But somehow she forgot all the techniques she'd learned, simply reveling in the feel and taste of him.

Time after time, she used her tongue to circle his head, loving the way it was so smooth on the top but slightly rougher at the bottom. And then there was his slit. It was now oozing freely and she felt something deep inside thrill at the response she had produced in him.

The books had all said the taste of come shouldn't be overwhelming in healthy men. But nowhere had she read that it could be addictive. Eliza knew she was becoming addicted to the taste of Clay on her tongue. Yet the most amazing thing was the way his increasing arousal was being telegraphed to her depths and doubling in its strength. She felt her juices redoubling and warming her inner lips.

"God, Liza. Stop or take more," he grunted. "You're killing me."

She stopped, unsure of herself. Could she be causing him pain? When she opened her mouth a bit more to ask, he pushed his cock into her mouth, and she took as much of his length as she could.

His answering moans of delight answered her question. He pounded himself into her mouth. She felt herself getting even hotter. She moved her head up and down on his shaft feeling his cock harden even further, and wrapped her tongue around the head to taste every inch of him.

Just when she was certain he was about to come again, he pulled away.

"Stop," he grunted.

She grinned mischievously and lowered her head again. He grabbed a clump of hair and pulled her back gently.

"No. This time, I'm going to be buried deep inside your beautiful cunt when I come. No substitutions."

She grinned. When he pushed her back against the rug, she went willingly. Soon she was lying on her back, her legs bent slightly. He fingered her pussy, rubbing her juices around her outer lips and then gently fingering her clit before moving between her legs. His cock entered her. She wanted nothing more than to feel every one of his nine hard inches, and just not an inch at a time. She reached for him trying to hurry things along.

"Oh, no," he muttered. "We're going to do this my way. That's a promise."

"Please, Clay," she cried. "Fuck me hard."

He placed his hands on her knees pushing them out against the rug and opening her even wider.

Another inch slid inside her. Eliza groaned and bit her bottom lip. Couldn't he tell he was driving her slowly insane? She tightened her muscles, trying to literally suck him deeper into her pussy. He laughed and held himself back.

"Not so fast, my sweet," he murmured against her ear. "Let's make this last until we both are screaming in ecstasy."

A warning bell rang distantly in her head. Those words sounded familiar. But when another inch of his incredibly hard shaft slid inside her, only to be withdrawn before she could react, all she could concentrate on was the riotous feelings racing through her.

She wrapped her legs tightly around his thighs, placed her hands on his butt and pulled with all her might. *Finally,* she thought as his full length thrust into her quivering pussy.

"Ah," she screamed as her innermost nerves exploded. She felt the jerking of his cock as he reached his own orgasm, his seed soaking her inner walls.

*　　　*　　　*

Eliza awoke with a slight feeling of disorientation. She was warm, her muscles as relaxed as they had ever been. There was a warm fire cracking and popping behind her and soft fur underneath her.

Lying on top of her, his cock starting to slowly expand inside her, was a hero worthy of any fantasy.

She opened her eyes and looked into the burning desire of the blue-black coals of his. His lips settled on hers and he began thrusting again. His cock moved easily, as their mixed body fluids began to heat. Her nerves, only seconds ago as pliant as cooked noodles, suddenly started to hum with desire. His tongue stroked inside her bottom lip, sucking gently and enticing her tongue to play.

They rocked together for long moments but their passion wouldn't be denied. Soon he was thrusting, harder and harder, and she was meeting each of his movements with an answering of her own, drawing him deeper inside her, wanting nothing more than to grab the glittering glow of satisfaction that hovered just out of her reach. When they rushed to the edge of the pinnacle and fell over it, Eliza felt tears build in her eyes at the beauty of the moment.

Just before she fell asleep a second time, she admitted to herself that she loved Clay Johnson. Perhaps that's why she dreamed he told her he loved her as well.

CHAPTER 4

When Eliza woke, she was alone and, for a moment, she thought everything had been nothing more than a wonderful, erotic dream. But the stickiness between her legs and sore muscles told her otherwise.

Still, she couldn't just lie on a bearskin rug naked and wait for her dream lover to return.

She got up and went in search of a bathroom. She found an unbelievable one with a whirlpool tub that she filled with the perfect temperature of water. When she finally eased into the bubbling, steamy water, she sighed in ecstasy. She leaned her head back against the warm, soft headrest and looked up at a huge moon-filled skylight. Funny, she'd never thought of Alaska as paradise, but right now, she couldn't imagine any place better in the world to be.

A small sound reached her and she turned her head. He came into the bathroom on nearly silent feet. He was wearing his jeans, top button unsnapped and his spectacular chest was bare. The jeans outlined every inch of his magnificent package. Eliza licked her lips in anticipation. Her eyes darted upward and widened at the sight he held in one hand, much like a waiter at a posh resort. He carried a silver tray laden with champagne, long stemmed glasses and a bowl of strawberries and whipped cream.

"I thought we could both use a little sustenance," he said, setting the tray on the edge of the tub then leaning over and taking her lips in a mind-numbing kiss.

"How did you know I've been dreaming of strawberries and

champagne?" Eliza asked when they finally parted.

"Oh, just lucky I guess." He poured her a flute of golden champagne, then poured one for him. Eliza watched the completely unconscious movements and felt a little thrill in her heart. It was all she could do not to pinch herself to make sure she wasn't dreaming. This was just like something out of one of Satin's books.

Suddenly, it hit Eliza. This entire trip was from a Satin book, "Alaskan Dreams." Eliza took another drink from her champagne while her thoughts raced. Was it coincidence or something else?

When he slid into the tub and moved toward her, a gleam in his eye, she gulped. Decisions, decisions. Should she just blurt her questions?

He took the glass from her nerveless fingers and took a sip from the exact spot where her lips had been. After one sip, he took another and lowered his head to her breast, suckling her nipple into his mouth. The contrast of her heated skin meeting the cool liquid in his mouth sent shock waves rippling through her. She wrapped her legs around his waist and felt his erect cock slide into her pussy. The position, her sitting on his lap allowed the length of her inner canal to measure him completely. She felt closer to him in every way than she had to any other person in her life.

She wrapped her arms around his neck threw back her head and let the sigh of ecstasy escape.

"God, you feel wonderful in my arms, Liza," he whispered against her neck. He placed his hands at her waist and lifted her slightly. She slid high on his cock then drifted downward again. Their sighs mingled on the steam-filled air. When the quivering of both their bodies slowed, he started to lift her again. This time she helped, using thigh muscles she thought woefully under-developed to lift herself higher. As his cock slipped from her, she clenched her pelvis muscles contracting against the tip of him and holding him steady. His eyelids lifted and she saw the gleam of surprised delight in his eyes.

"Trying to take control here, little one?" he asked.

"Not really," she answered on a gasp as he flexed his own hips and surged deeper inside her. With her clenched inner muscles, the movement seemed to make him feel even larger, if possible.

She rolled her pelvis a touch and felt the spasms of his cock in response. She didn't care who was in control and who wasn't at this point. All that mattered was getting this man as close to her as possible.

She lowered her head and met his lips, their tongues dancing and dueling in delight. His hands fitted around her hips, lifted her then slammed her back down against his own pelvis. When her quivering had almost died down, Clay trailed a finger down her butt before inserting it along the length of his cock stretching her inner muscles to a fullness she wouldn't have believed possible. She felt her release start deep inside and moaned into his mouth. Her gasp met his and, just before her vision went black, Liza knew he was following her over the edge into ecstasy.

*   *   *

Liza didn't know how long it took for her to come back to her senses. It could have been minutes, but since the relaxed muscles in her legs were starting to go a bit numb, she doubted it. What she did know was that Clay was still holding her on his lap and his cock was still buried inside her. Although not hard, it was a long way from flaccid. A little tensing of her pussy walls sparked a satisfying outcome.

"God, woman," he growled. "Are you trying to kill me?"

She laughed and looked into his beautiful, sparkling eyes. She saw humor, desire and above all, satisfaction there. The same thing she was sure he could see in her eyes.

"You know, even studs like Fabio get a break every now and then." He moved one hand and patted her lightly on the butt then slowly disengaged them. "I need something to eat before we go another round."

Liza straightened her shoulders. Time to have it out. This latest comment about Fabio, the hero in Satin's last book, could no longer be considered a coincidence. Something was definitely up.

"What do you know about Fabio?"

Clay sat back against the edge of the whirlpool. "Fabio? W-e-l-l-l-l, he's a fictional character."

"I know that. How do you know it?"

Clayton shrugged. If Liza didn't know better she'd almost think he was blushing.

"I don't know. I must've heard of him somewhere." He started moving again. "Let me go to the kitchen and see if I can't rustle us up some real grub. We'll save the strawberries for dessert." He leered playfully and added, "You've got to be hungry as well."

"Not so fast, buster." Liza grabbed Clayton by his pride and held on. She was momentarily diverted when it immediately reacted, rising to attention, but forged ahead.

"Have you been violating my private work space and going through my computer at work?"

"Uh, well, you know. The company computers are not your private space. It clearly states that in the employee handbooks."

"Don't give me that, mister. Those books were on cds I brought from home. They are for my personal use."

Clayton shook his head. "Not when you're using them on company time. For Christ's sake, Eliza, that's erotic romance you were reading. Stories by Satin Plesure, a famous erotic romance author. Not just one but dozens of erotic romances on the computer. On my dime."

Eliza straightened her shoulders. "I wasn't reading..." She clapped a hand over her mouth, appalled at what she had been about to say.

"I know," he interrupted. "You were writing them. You are Satin Pleasure, queen of erotic romance writers."

"Oh, boy," Eliza murmured. "You found out my little secret."

"Little? My God, Eliza, what were thinking? Don't you realize one of the boys in tech services could've discovered the same thing I did when they did regular maintenance on your machine?"

"But I was careful. Everything I did was on cds and floppy disks."

"Come on, Eliza. That isn't an excuse. Everything you put on a computer can be traced. It's almost worse than a paper trail. What would people think if they found out my executive assistant was writing erotic romances between taking dictation and typing minutes of board meetings?"

"Oh." Eliza bit the inside of her lip. She really hadn't considered that. Her shoulders slumped. "I wasn't doing it while I was taking dictation. I was only doing it on my lunch and coffee breaks."

"Oh, well, that's much better. Whatever happened to actually eating lunch and drinking coffee?"

Eliza stuck her chin out. This was ridiculous. "You know, Clayton, the way you're carrying on about this is silly. I think you're jealous. I think that's what this is really all about."

Clay stepped toward her. Though the water in the tub was still frothing gently, Eliza felt like she was a dingy being tossed about in a hurricane from the heat of his gaze as it stroked over her. She felt her nipples harden and couldn't help but notice that he was getting just as aroused as she.

"You're damn right I'm jealous. All this time, I've been keeping things just business between us. All this time, I've been doing my damnedest to keep my hands off of you."

"Did I ever ask you to keep things perfectly business? Did I?"

Clayton ran a hand over his face. "No, but that's not the point."

"What *is* the point?"

"The point is how can a normal man compete with an erotic romance writer's fantasies?"

Eliza felt her anger dissolve at the entreaty in his eyes.

She took his hand in hers and held it against her breast. It was a good hand, strong and tanned, but ever so gentle.

"Don't you understand, Clay? You don't need to compete with my fantasies. They're all about you. You inspired every hero Satin has ever created." She brought his hand to her lips and kissed it gently. "You're my dream lover, my dream boss, my fantasy man."

He pulled her into his arms and sealed her vow with his lips. Long moments later they pulled apart. She lay her head against his chest and felt the reassuring beat of his heart.

"Well, now that is settled, there are still a few things I need to do."

She looked up at him. "Yeah, I know. You need food. I'll help. We probably should get everything ready for your meetings this weekend. I can't believe we're still the only ones to arrive so far."

As she stepped from the tub, she looked back at Clay and caught the sheepish look on his face. "There aren't any meetings, are there?"

He bit his bottom lip and looked sideways.

"Well, hell, why did you go to all the trouble to make this look like a business trip?" she asked incredulously.

"You have to remember I was trying to compete with the men in Satin's books. None of them would have just said, 'Come on baby, let's go make love.' They're heroic, they're suave, they're sexy. They're romantic."

"And so are you," she said, wrapping her arms around his neck. "So are you."

They hugged and kissed passionately. Long minutes later they parted and she asked, "But why go to all of this trouble? You could've just asked me out."

He looked down at her. "Well, I was going to then I happened to read "Alaskan Dreams." I recognize a superior idea when I see one."

Eliza started laughing. "That you do. Let's go get something to eat." She took his hand and pulled him from the whirlpool.

"By the way, you might be interested in some research I did recently," she said as they headed for the kitchen. "It involves sundaes and hot fudge..."

MOLDING CLAY

———————————————

CHAPTER 1

"I'll let you represent me if you come to my house and spend the next forty-eight hours doing anything I say. If you're still able to walk out my door, I'll sign the contract."

The statement hung in the air surrounding them for three complete heartbeats.

"So? How about it? You're an entrepreneur, right? You built an art empire from nothing. Are you willing to put it all on the line?"

Clay Fife looked at the fey creature standing in front of him.

She was Edith Agnes Raines and should have been a little, old lady wearing support hose and wildly flowered dresses. She was anything but dumpy, even if she was dressed like no woman he'd ever seen. Before he'd ever met her, this woman had been haunting him.

Now she taunted his male pride.

"I can't believe you want to make this bet," Clay said.

She smiled. It was like a hungry feline looking at a breakfast mouse. At six-foot-four-and-a-half inches tall and two-hundred-twenty pounds, Clay wasn't used to feeling like a mouse.

"Why? Don't tell me you're one of those men who thinks only they can make the first move?"

"Of course not," Clay asserted. "I will admit I've never had an artist respond this way when I've offered to bring their work to the world."

"It seems you've been dealing with the wrong kind of artists then, Mr. Fife."

Clay laughed. He realized he felt more alive in this moment than he had in more than a decade. "Surely, since you've offered to let me screw you senseless for two days, you can call me Clay."

Her smile drooped. "Please, there's no need to be crass."

"Why pretty it up? If that's not bargaining for sex, I don't know what is." He stepped forward a bit. This was more like it. He could see some of her bravado fading. He was certain if he pushed a little more he'd get what he wanted.

He wanted her talent in his galleries and her body in his bed. By damn, he would have both—on his terms, not hers.

She wasn't beautiful. Not in the classic sense at least. Though short and a little round, it was a roundness that appealed to him on all levels.

Had he been of the right mind, he could have called any of a dozen women he'd escorted in the past five years who were all more beautiful than Edith Raines. Some of those women were the most often photographed faces in the world. At this point, he couldn't recall what even one of them looked like. All he could see in his mind's eye was Edith, with her fiery red hair and hazel green eyes.

He tried to analyze why she so attracted him. Her clothes weren't what you'd see the average woman on the street wearing. Most artists didn't dress normal, though, and he'd never been attracted to any of the more flamboyant ones.

Edith was dressed like a cross between a biker babe and a jock. She wore black leather pants that followed every curve of her legs as faithfully as a Harley would a curving strip of asphalt. The pants were floodwater high, almost capri length, but that was okay because he got a glimpse of trim, little ankles at the end of those short legs. He could see a braided bracelet around one ankle. It wasn't gold or silver like a gift from an attentive lover, but appeared to be made from some gaily-colored glass beads like those found in a child's play art set.

On tiny feet that looked equally childlike to him, she wore ancient flip-flops showcasing ten toenails, each polished a different color.

Above the leather pants and flip-flops she wore a faded football jersey. Even though it engulfed her, he could tell she wasn't wearing a bra. When he looked at her like he was now, the nipples of her full, lush breasts beaded in response. Yes, when he had tamed this tiger kitten, he'd love spending the rest of this millennium curled into her body, making love and drowning in the feast she offered.

He'd do it with her on top, with him on top, from behind, doggy-style. Hell, he'd screw every orifice of her plush, little body.

He almost groaned aloud at the thought of pumping his nine inches up her ass, then pulling out and shooting his load over what he was betting were plump cheeks of gold.

First, though, he had to handle the bet and business.

"So if you don't want sex, what do you want?" He pushed a little harder verbally. In his experience, people who tried to best him always backed down under pressure.

"I didn't say I didn't want to…" She paused.

Clay hid his grin. Little Miss Edith wasn't quite the bohemian she was portraying. She couldn't even say the word.

"…screw you. I just wanted you to understand that not everything on this earth can be bought with your money and reputation."

Clay laughed out loud. Oh, this was fun. Laughing was a good cover. Because the way she'd lingered over the word screw, her cupid bow's mouth rounding on the "r-e-w," he could picture those lips wrapped around his… No, better not go there or he'd forget all about business.

Still it was good to feel the blood rushing to that certain part of his body again, especially after what happened the last time he'd been with a sexy woman.

Funny, he was only forty-seven. He'd never thought he'd have to see a doctor for that particular problem, even when he reached eighty. The quack he'd visited, a doctor he'd only previously seen on the golf course, had shrugged it off as stress and told Clay to take a vacation, while he was stealing five hundred beans by acing the gimme shot on the seventeenth green.

Clay had smarted more over the crack about a vacation than the money. A holiday was precisely how he'd ended up in tiny Youngstown, New York, on the banks of the Niagara River.

In the forty-eight hours he'd been here, Clay had been certain of two things. One: he'd never again listen to a doctor who could easily turn to the professional golf tour. Two: he hated vacations.

His soon-to-be-ex secretary had probably been part of the ruse. She's the one who had rented him a cabin. He almost shuddered at the thought. *A cabin, for God's sake.* He was a man who never stayed in anything less than a five-star hotel on the concierge level.

This place was rustic to the max. It had a wonderful view, standing as it did on a rocky ledge overlooking the Niagara River. It even reminded him, briefly, of his native Scotland. He'd enjoyed the view and silence accompanying said view for all of fifteen minutes. Then he'd longed for the lights and action of Manhattan.

Or the frenetic pace of Paris.

Or the understated elegance of Milan.

Hell, now that he'd spent forty-eight hours of his vacation here, he'd even settle for one of the casinos in nearby Niagara Falls or the towny bars on Chippewa Street in Buffalo, which he'd read about in the Chamber of Commerce brochures that passed for the only decent reading material in the cabin.

He hadn't resorted to picking up any of the dozens of romance novels scattered about—although the covers had been interesting.

There would be no action for him, though. He was stuck in Youngstown without a car or Internet for ten more days.

When he was inside the cabin, it was even worse. It wasn't a shack. In fact, the furnishings were nice if you went in for the tradition of solid American Oak and the Quaker style. He'd liked the feel of the solid wood under his body. Maybe when he got back to his apartment in Manhattan he'd have a decorator come in and remove the New Age crap he'd let his last lover talk him into and get something closer to these furnishings.

But nice as the furnishings were, it simply wouldn't do. It had an ancient gas stove for cooking and a fireplace you had to chop the wood for. It seemed the plumbing only ran to ice cold and tepid water, and, although the completely glassed-in back wall of the shower that looked out over the forest behind the cabin was a surreal touch, there wasn't a whirlpool tub or even multiple shower heads like he favored.

The thing about the cabin that truly was driving him insane had nothing to do with the aesthetics, and yet everything to do with them.

Quite simply…the place smelled of lavender, lace and honey.

There were knickknacks everywhere. It was quaint; it was homey. He could see old Edith Agnes sitting in a rocking chair, her support hose around her ankles and knitting serenely.

So why did just walking into the place give him a woody that standing under an icy shower for fifteen minutes hadn't helped. Neither did the hand job he'd resorted to this morning. Before he'd even finished dressing, he'd had a boner again.

Where had old Samson the faithful been when he'd entertained those three models in Florence last month? Instead, Sammy boy was ready to go while he was staying in an old maid's cabin and there wasn't a decent or legal hole in sight for him to plug. At least that's what Clay had been thinking when he'd walked into the town that morning.

That was until he'd turned off the quaint Main Street. The jade sculpture had been sitting in the front window of a tiny, unassuming art store. It had stolen his breath. Then, moments later, when he'd stormed inside to buy the piece, its creator had done it again.

Now he also knew the cause of his cabinitis. She was his landlord and it was her essence inside the cabin driving him slowly mad.

She was an artist so that meant she automatically marched to the beat of a different drummer. Obviously it didn't take much to live here, but when he considered that a showing in any of his galleries was guaranteed to bring the artist upwards of eight figures, she should be jumping all over his offer. Instead, she was acting as if he'd offered her his dirty Jockeys.

If this was just a coy act to get his commission lowered, it wasn't going to work. He'd wait until after the next forty-eight hours to tell her that. No sense ruining the fun and games he had in store for them before it was necessary.

He smiled and took tremendous pleasure at how quickly her look of triumph faded from her face.

"You want to do this here?" he asked glancing around at her tiny store.

"Er, no. I live right behind the cabin you rented. Just go through the woods," she said.

He nodded and smiled. When she took a step back, he felt even stronger than before.

"You've got a deal," he purred. "I'll be at your place at six tonight." He strode out the door.

*   *   *

Edi sank down on the stool behind her cash register and put shaking hands over her face. She knew it was just her imagination that it felt as if all the air had rushed out of the tiny storefront with his departure. This was her home, her sanctuary, her way of connecting with people without any of the dangers. It had been for nearly ten years now. She didn't have any pretensions here and didn't want them. This was exactly what she wanted, a small store that sold what she wanted, when she wanted.

"What have I done?" she murmured. The answer was short and succinct. She'd made a bargain with the devil and now she had to deal with the consequences.

Well, she'd handled bigger deals than this in her lifetime and, she smiled to herself, with nowhere near the potential for fun. Edi ran her hand through her shaggy hair. The funny thing was she knew Clay.

Well, knew might be too strong a word. She knew of him. How could a woman forget the man who had ruined her and changed the entire course of her life? She also knew something about him that went deeper than just business, something few other people knew. She had no doubt, however, that he was clueless about her.

In 1991, determined to make a go of things in the art world, she had put everything she had on the line in an attempt to buy a small SoHo gallery out from under a corporation determined to buy it, close it and sell the land to a developer. What followed was a nasty takeover attempt including lawyers, finance men and tense moments. Neither she nor the corporation knew Fife was waiting in the wings. It was the old shell game magnified by twenty-million dollars. While she was fighting one enemy and seeming to win, Fife had done an end-run and beaten them both at the game. The corporation of McGovern & McGovern had walked away with nothing more than hurt pride. Edi had walked away broke and on the street.

Even though she'd turned to her art and made her way back on her own terms, Edi had never forgotten the lessons she'd learned that fateful afternoon.

Nor had she forgotten the man who'd taught them.

The years had been kind to him. He was older certainly. Although they had never met personally, she'd seen his picture then. He'd had ink-black hair and snapping blue eyes. There were touches of grey now, winging through the black at his crown and edging a bit at the short, neat sideburns. But the eyes were just as vivid and just as full of life.

When the rental agent had contacted her about the temporary contract on her cabin, she'd said the client needed to get a break for his health. But Clay had looked pretty healthy to her today standing toe-to-toe with her in her shop.

For a second she had another moment of apprehension, but she firmed her resolve. There was one goal here and she would attain it.

Over a decade ago, he had been the teacher. Before the weekend was over, she would return the favor. Perhaps, too, she'd be able to chill the anger she had felt all those years ago. The anger she thought had cooled long ago, but had risen to the surface when he stalked into her store like he was king of the world.

Well, if he was a king, it wasn't here. Here she was the boss, the one who held all the marbles. She had something he wanted, did she? It would take more than just waving his magic checkbook this time.

*   *   *

Clay shrugged his shoulders and tried to contain the nervous shiver running down his spine. There was no reason to be nervous. This wasn't a date. It wasn't a courtship.

It wasn't like he was a virgin. Hell, neither he nor his lovers had been virgins for more years than he could count.

It was business.

He certainly wasn't a virgin at that either.

Still, he ran his finger around the collar of his shirt as he stood outside the front door of her house.

House was really a misnomer. It was a barn and stood not more than five-hundred yards away from his cabin. Of course, the overgrown forest was a good boundary line, but if he'd known this was where he'd find the illusive Edith, he'd have braved the wilds much sooner.

She signed her work E.A. Raines. Something about the name rang a bell, but he couldn't put his finger on it. Jesus, it was like he had the early stages of Alzheimer's or something, the way he couldn't remember things these days.

She didn't look like an E.A., which sounded like someone who wears short, black skirts, medium high heels and sucked down whiskey sours and business deals with equal abandon.

Neither, after meeting her, did Edith really fit with the picture. Edith was that old lady he'd first imagined, content to sit and rock the hours away on the porch of a quaint cabin.

Neither E.A. nor Edith was the type of woman to give him a constant woody. The woman he'd met earlier today was Edith Agnes.

Edith Agnes was sultry, suggestive and unconventional. Edith Agnes would keep him on his toes and that's what Clay wanted in life. It was what he'd always sought.

Clay had made his first fortune in imports and exports. Maybe some of them hadn't been legal, but that was in the past now.

He'd turned to the art world because he wanted to prove to himself that he could conquer it on some level. It had been a dream of his mother, and his own fantasy as well, to see his work hanging in a gallery. Dreams and fantasies didn't pay the bills, especially when his work had been panned as thoroughly as fool's gold. He could still remember the art teacher's scorn when Clay had produced his masterpiece. "Don't quit your day job," had been the man's pithy words of wisdom.

Clay had taken them to heart, but had also set his mind to making sure he never squashed an artist's dreams in quite the same way. There was no arguing, though, that once he turned his efforts to selling art rather than creating it, the money had started flowing like water down a cliff.

In the past six months, as Clay had brought another artist fame and fortune, the longing to pick up a brush was starting to stir again. He'd put aside the longing as he had for the last fifteen years. He knew what he was good at and it wasn't painting. It was discovering new talent and selling their work. He saw it all as a big game, one he rarely lost. For the first dozen years, the high of winning was like nothing else he'd ever known.

He didn't know when exactly, he just knew he felt weary and old, much beyond the forty-seven years he'd lived. When had the joy of the game of art gone from his life? When had the game become a job?

He wouldn't think about the past or the future. He'd think about the present.

Clay raised his fist to knock on the huge wooden door and stopped when he felt a tingle run from his neck down his spine. He turned. She was standing to his left, watching him. If he could have pushed his breath out of his lungs, he would have whistled. As it was all he could do was stare.

She was wearing a white terry cloth towel wrapped sarong-style with a knot tied just above her breasts. He could see a small half-moon shaped birthmark above the right one. He had a sudden, overwhelming urge to taste that birthmark. His tongue shivered at the thought.

"You're over-dressed," she said, breaking him from the intense waking dream holding him immobile. "Get undressed and put this on. Then come around back." She handed him a towel and walked away.

He gulped at the way the outfit she was wearing followed the line of her spine and the curve of her ass. As she walked, he saw hints of the shadows of her ass cheeks.

He grinned, put the items he held on the porch, then began tugging off his shirt and pants. She thought he was overdressed, eh? He could rectify that. There was no one around for miles and if she wanted to get up close and personal with nature, who was he to argue? He'd figured they'd drink a little wine and talk first, but, hey, he was nothing if not adaptable.

In seconds, he was naked except for the towel around his waist. He picked up the bottle of champagne—no sense wasting prime booze—and a single yellow rose out of the dozen he'd brought with him. He had a fantasy about stroking the rose over each of her nipples, then suckling the turgid point until she cried out her pleasure.

Being inside the cabin wasn't necessary to his plan. He could do it just as easily outside.

He rounded the corner and stopped cold. She had a pedestal sitting in the late summer sunshine. In front of it was a low table in front of a short stool. A potter's wheel with a large clump of clay sat at the ready. Clay frowned. He realized now, as she moved away, she wasn't wearing a towel at all, but a white terrycloth sarong.

Before, he'd felt decidedly over-dressed. Now he felt under-dressed.

"Come on, chop, chop," she said. "We've only got a few hours more of sunlight."

"You want me to pose for you?" he asked. He hoped she wouldn't realize how strangled his voice sounded.

"Yes."

"I didn't realize that was on the agenda for tonight." He was proud. There was definitely no sign of nerves in his voice now.

"Well, I can't be responsible for what you thought was going to happen here. I'm only responsible for my thoughts."

"Look, although I'm flattered at the…" He paused a moment, searching for the right word. It was while he was doing his mental searching that he realized it was all she could do to keep from laughing out loud. He frowned.

"Most people would call it a compliment," she provided helpfully.

"Yes, most would. However, I'm not most people. I thought you understood that."

She smiled and he lost his ability to breathe again. "I do. Maybe you realize now that I'm not most people either."

He laughed. "Believe me, I realized that within five seconds of meeting you."

He should have felt odd wearing nothing but a towel while she was dressed and while they discussed personality traits. All Clay felt was more interested than ever.

"Anyway," she continued, "we really don't have time to discuss your philosophy of compliments. We're losing the light. Sit on the stool and relax."

He crossed his arms over his chest. "No. I don't pose for artists.

Ever."

"Not even for one you want to sign with your gallery?"

"Not even for her. I'll go get my clothes and then let's go somewhere civilized and discuss this whole thing like rational adults."

"No."

Clay frowned. "No?"

"No. You're not going anywhere. We have a bet or have you forgotten already? If you leave, I win the bet much easier than I anticipated."

Clay shook his head. "Look, Edith, time for fun and games is over. Let's stop this nonsense and get on with our business. Once that's settled, we can move to the really important subject of just how often you're going to let me screw you."

Edith laughed. It wasn't a reassuring sound.

"Oh, I had you all wrong, Clay. I had you pegged as a gambler. I didn't think a little thing like posing nude for me was going to send you scurrying like a scared, little boy." Edith laughed again and this time she stalked slowly towards him. "Oh, you have a reputation for being such a killer. I've found out the truth and all it took was a little pressure in the right place."

She paused and ran one finger, just one, down his arm from his elbow to his wrist. His skin prickled with heat at the touch. He couldn't hide that reaction, but he did narrow his eyes.

"Don't count your winnings quite so fast," he said, turning the arm she was touching and clamping his hand around her small wrist. "Where do you want me?"

She smiled again. This one wasn't quite so predatory, but it did have a bit more of the smugness of victory than he'd like. Still, it was early in the game. He was content to let her think she'd won. At least for now.

CHAPTER 2

Clay sat on the stool in the sunlight. The towel was still around his waist covering his private parts. She hadn't said to take it off and he wasn't about to offer. He'd finally figured out what game she was playing. She wanted to have control. Well, she'd have to fight for every inch she won. He'd be patient, cunning. Before she knew what hit her, he'd have wrested the control away and she'd be happy about it.

She sat behind her potter's wheel. The sound of the wheel turning and birds in the tops of the trees surrounded them.

He just sat in the sun watching her. The wheel was turning the clay at a steady pace and she was using both her hands and her cutting blade with cunning precision. For all the sculptures he had sold in his career, he'd never really watched an artist at work. He told himself it was because he didn't have the time, but, in truth, watching someone create something amazing from nothing was just too damn hard. It reminded him of all the things that could never be.

Watching Edith, however, was hypnotizing. He knew he should be staring her down, trying to force his will on her, but he couldn't take his eyes off her hands. They were long and supple, which shouldn't have looked right on her body type. They looked more than right. He could almost close his eyes and see the beauty of her hands as they molded and shaped the clay to her will.

He felt a stirring in his body and tried again to focus his mind on other things. He looked away momentarily. It didn't seem to help. The picture was imbedded in his mind and suddenly he felt as if she were actually touching him, molding him as if he were the lump of clay.

His heartbeat sped up and he felt a fine sheen of sweat breaking out on his chest and upper arms. It's just hot sitting in the sun, he rationalized. He looked again at Edith. The clay in her hands was beginning to take shape. He could see the outline of a curved ass and a long back of a male body's shape rising from the base.

God, the clay back wasn't the only thing rising out of a lump. The dreamy, sexy look on her face as she worked at her art was arousing him like nothing he'd ever known. He could tell there was a flush working its way up her chest above her wrap, heating the tops of her breasts a rosy red and darkening the birthmark. He wanted to go to her, pull her against him and take her standing up. Right there, right now.

Samson responded with amazing agility. He rose to his full height, making an impressive tent in the towel Clay was wearing.

Edith's eyes were on him. They caressed his chest, following the line of hair as it went between his nipples and down to his belly button. When she saw the evidence Samson was displaying in proud bounty, her eyes widened. Almost as if against her will, she licked her lips.

Clay groaned. "Come to me, Edith." His voice sounded strained to him. No surprise. The way Samson was acting it was a wonder he could even talk.

She shook her head slowly and licked her lips again. His groan became even more painful.

"Then, honey, stop looking at me like that," he said quietly.

"Like what?" she replied.

"Like you want me to ride you like a stallion does a mare."

Edith smiled. This was another one of those smiles that made him feel like he was that mouse again. Strangely, it didn't deflate Samson. It just caused him to strain a little closer to the edge of the towel. Clay didn't have to look down to know his tip was probably poking out through the slit where the two ends of the cloth met just above his groin.

"Perhaps it'll be the mare who rides the stallion," she said.

Clay felt his heart skip a beat.

She slowly worked her hands over and around the clay, as it spun slowly on the pedestal. She was molding it, shaping it to her will. Clay felt each stroke, every press and push against mud, as if her fingers were stroking down his skin, as if she were molding his muscles to her will as well.

Instead of feeling used and powerless, he felt empowered. He wanted to be shaped by her. He needed her to feel him and be pleased by what moved beneath her touch.

Even though he knew it wasn't precisely what he'd originally wanted, Clay could no longer sit still. He didn't think of it as letting her control him or keeping the upper hand. Every nerve ending in his body seemed to be jumping through his skin, doing its best to get to her, to actually feel those magnificent, artistic hands kneading his skin.

He stood and, in three quick steps, he was at her side. He knelt beside her and wrapped his arms around her waist, pulling her against him. Her hip nudged against his cock and when her lips met his, he sighed his relief. They were full, sweet and hot, like warm caramel melting over cold ice cream. He had a moment's fantasy of covering her in caramel and licking it off, uncovering her skin inch by inch.

That fantasy was for later. Her lips parted and his tongue sought entry inside her mouth. The sweetness continued there, along with a little tartness when her teeth nipped at his tongue. The slight pain sent him into a further spin on the ride of desire. When her tongue met his and a slow dance ensued, Clay knew he could happily spend forever kissing and exploring her mouth.

Her hands left the clay and begin moving over his chest. He felt the coolness of the clay on her fingers as they traced over his pectorals. When they spun around his nipples, he groaned as his desire trilled higher.

Her hands trailed lower over his stomach and down to where the towel was barely staying around his hips. One touch and the cloth parted, and he finally knew what it felt like for her cool fingers to stroke against his aching tip.

"God, Edith," he groaned, "please."

She laughed. The sound sent shivers over his skin.

"Oh, I intend to more than please," she said before her lips swooped to take his own again.

She was the aggressor this time and he was swept away in the storm surge of her passion. Bites followed by soothing strokes, tongues parrying and dancing much like the thrust of a cock into a pussy. Lips fused as if they would never be parted.

Clay lost track of how long they kissed. He knew at some point they would have to come up for air or die. At the moment, dying was preferable because he didn't want to give up the taste or the feel of her against him. He also knew that, no matter what, he would not be able to survive without tasting her again and often.

His hands, greedy to get some of the action his mouth was enjoying, stroked over her skin. He started at the ball of her shoulder and worked his way slowly down her arm. She was soft, so soft. He continued the exploration. The hair on her arm was soft and fine like a baby's. When he passed his hand a bit above it, the hairs quivered and rose to meet his touch, as if drawn by a magnetic lure they couldn't resist. When he reached the strong wrist, well used to the strenuous motions of her art, he could feel the way her pulse raced beneath the skin.

His lips curved slightly against hers. There was being in control and then there was being controlled. He didn't know who was what, but he knew this battle was going to be one with no true loser. Almost regretfully, he trailed his hand back up her arm to her shoulder again. She was small and slight despite the strength he knew the curves hid. He could keep his pinky on her shoulder joint and spread his hand and touch the beginning of the cleavage between her breasts. Her quick indrawn breath made his smile grow.

He pulled his lips from hers and worked his way down her neck. His goal was those breasts. Her breathing was quick, short gasps of pleasure. When his mouth touched the small indentation at the base of her throat, he felt her pulse spike again. He bit, then suckled there for a few seconds bringing the taste of lavender and honey fully into his senses. He moved lower and did the same thing to the top of her left breast, then her right, using his tongue to trace the half-moon on its crest. She caught her breath when he tongued, then bit at it gently.

His hands joined his mouth and he loosened her sarong, baring all of her.

Those breasts he had only dreamed and fantasized about were better than he had imagined. Full and pouting slightly, they were creamy white mounds. He put his hand under each one and lifted them higher for a better inspection and taste. He had forgotten what it felt like when breasts more than filled his large hands. His last few lovers had been small to the point of non-existent up top. No wonder he hadn't been able to feel any desire for them. These were breasts of a woman. These were meant for heaven.

His hands started high on her stomach and moved upward, stroking and caressing the underside of each and he allowed his pinkies to graze just the bottom edge of her areolas. They were a deep plum color and he promised himself he would soon taste them as well.

For now, he limited his mouth and lips to stinging love bites across the tops of her beasts. The vanilla was stronger here and was the greatest aphrodisiac he had ever known.

She shivered in response, and Clay's muscles quivered as if everything he was feeling was coming back to him magnified several hundred times.

When her hands, which had been moving like a feather over his tip, encircled his rod fully, the desire racing through him spilled out on a groan.

Her thumb and index fingers wound around his base and acted like the most effective cock ring in the world. Clay lost it a little. He pulled her forward, off the bench and into his lap and thrust deep inside her.

"God, you're tight," he grunted when he finally could get a word out between his gasping breaths. She fit him like a tight leather glove. He could feel each tremor of her inner muscles as she flexed and relaxed against him.

"God, you're huge," she whispered back.

He laughed, then groaned when she ground her mouth against his and rolled her hips. Had he thought before he had been as deep as possible inside her? He knew better now as another inch of him slid inside her warm velvet canal. Her fingers were still around his base, but now they were trapped against her labia and his groin. She must have bent her index finger at the knuckle because suddenly he felt the scrape of her short nail against his skin.

He could feel his cock swelling and widening. His balls were so full they were about to split. How was it possible? He was forty-seven years old. He hadn't lost his control this quickly since his first time in the alley with a prostitute when he was fifteen. He was determined he would keep control in this at least. But he could feel it slipping from his grasp as the haze of passion and need rode through his body and washed over him like a tidal flood.

"Edith," he started, trying to search the marshmallow that was his brain for some word to slow things down.

Edith rolled her hips again and this time she straightened her index finger so it was stretched alongside his cock inside her warm canal.

"Come on…fuck me hard," she said, biting him on his nipple.

That little sting of pain sent him over the edge.

He grabbed her by the hips and held her against him—not that she was trying to get away from him—but something animalistic in him refused to take any chance she'd stop this. He pounded inside her as his cum jettisoned out like it was fired from a rocket launcher.

She didn't shrink from his physical attack. In fact, she ground herself harder against him, as if she wanted to become part of his skin. That was fine with him. He could feel her vaginal walls milking him and that was even more of a turn-on. His cock swelled, even as it continued to jerk with his release.

In the past, when he'd taken the edge of his passion off, he'd been able to back off a little and extend his lover's pleasure for at least an hour longer. But Edith wasn't like any of his past lovers. What she did to him was beyond anything he'd ever known. The only thing that remained in his mind and soul was the need to mark this woman as his through all time. So he thrust.

Harder and harder. Sharper and sharper.

It was territorial. It was primal.

Somewhere, sounding like a sound off in the distance beyond the plain of earth, Clay heard a cry.

Was it pain? Was it her? God he hoped not, but it didn't matter since he couldn't stop. A gasping groan escaped his mouth as his vision blurred. It couldn't go on much longer. He couldn't go on.

But he couldn't stop. When she fought a little, bucking her pelvis against his own, his heart nearly stopped.

Was she fighting him? Was he really hurting her?

"Damn you," she muttered. "Don't you dare stop now! I'm so verrry close!"

The passion overtook him completely. He thrust so deep and hard inside her he thought her inner muscles must be splitting from his pounding. His cock was so hard it hurt. In the last moment, when he thought he would pass out, he released control and his load shot out of him again in long, cleansing jerks.

He took a deep breath ready to just go to sleep and opened his eyes. The look of pain on her face at being so close to release but denied sent him back over the edge. With what was surely his last breath, he curled his lips around her nipple and bit as gently as he could. As his cock was still spasmaming inside her, he inserted his index finger through the top folds of her pussy and found her hard, swollen clit. One stroke was all it took and her release shattered over them both. Her scream of satisfaction bounced through the clearing.

He must have passed out for a few seconds because, when he became aware of things again, Clay realized she was curled against his lap like a well-satisfied kitten, alternately licking and kissing everywhere on his chest she could reach.

"Hhhmmm," she purred.

"Hhhmmm, is right," he answered. His cock was shrinking a bit, but she still held him deep inside her. He could feel their come starting to follow the path of gravity. It hit him suddenly. They hadn't used any protection.

She could be pregnant.

Clay waited for the panic to overwhelm him. Seconds passed. No panic, just sheer contentment. *Maybe it would be a boy. Or perhaps it would be a girl with Edith's curls.*

"Well, you promised me a ride and you delivered. I didn't know Scottish stallions were bred quite that strong," she said, patting him on the shoulder.

He laughed. This wasn't a laughing matter. But when he looked into her gleaming, satisfied eyes, he knew there was a lot of laughing ahead of them.

"I didn't wear a rubber." He cursed under his breath when he saw the light fade from her eyes. Why hadn't he said that with a little more finesse or just kept quiet?

"Well, no. If you had posed a little longer instead of taking the bull by the horns, I'd have suggested we retire to the house. I had a package of condoms there." She took a breath. Before he could say the words his heart was urging, she continued, "But don't worry. I'm on the pill. Of course, you could give me something. Have you been checked lately?"

Clay felt his hackles rise. "I'm healthy as a horse."

"There are those farm animal references again. Are you sure you weren't raised in the country?"

"Certain. Ever been to Scotland?"

"No." She patted him on the sweaty shoulder.

It was friendly, chummy even. For some reason he didn't want to focus on, that annoyed the hell out of him.

"Come on and move, big boy. I think we both need to cool off."

He rose and turned back to her house, telling himself the noise their bodies made when they separated wasn't miraculously turning him on again. It took a moment to realize she was walking in the other direction.

"Aren't we going in the house?" he asked.

"No, I think we need something a little more au naturale," she said. "When was the last time you went skinny dipping?"

Clay paused. "A lifetime ago."

Edith smiled and it nearly took his breath again. "Well, I think tonight is definitely reason to end the streak. Follow me."

She led the way through the woods behind her house. The path was not quite wide enough for them to walk side-by-side. That was all right because Clay got to watch her tremendous ass as it moved in front of him. He had another fantasy of taking her that way and felt Samson stirring in earnest again. Well, if he still had any doubts after his earlier performance with Edith, he now had proof positive he'd have no need for those old man pills the doctor had given him.

They rounded a slight bend in the path and the Niagara River sprawled in front of them. They were standing on a small rocky beach. It was protected on one side by a long finger of wooded land sticking about a hundred yards into the river. On the other was the slope of a cliff that shot two hundred feet into the sky. The sun hung low in the western sky. For a moment, Clay knew this place had looked the exact way for a thousand years.

But a flash of movement to his left startled him from his reprieve.

"Last one in, rotten egg," she called gaily as she ran forward, splashing through the waves.

He had never been called a slow learner in his life. He wouldn't be one now.

As her laughter trailed after her in the dying light of day, he felt as if he were shedding a hundred pounds of weariness. Catching her would be a snap. He was quicker and bigger. But there was something to be said for letting the game run a slower course. Patience would win him the same outcome. Yes, he had a feeling before the weekend was through, he'd get everything he desired.

Clay lost track of how long they played. It was like a ballet in silky smooth water that caressed his skin and worked like magic fingers of relaxation on his entire body. She ran and he chased.

He ran and she chased.

A hand on the foot led to an intimate game of footsy. Her toes kneading his cock as she floated on her back away from him, his foot floating against her pussy while his toes flexed gently just inside her outer walls and the water wrapped them in cool comfort.

When he caught her fully against him the first time, she wrapped her arms around his neck and smiled at him. The brush of her body against his was arousing, but also comforting in a way he hadn't expected. She moved her mouth close to his and he smiled as he awaited her kiss. Her tongue traced slowly along his lips, as if licking the taste of him and the water from his skin. His body began to heat and his eyelids lowered, anticipating the rush of tasting her again.

But instead of a kiss, he felt the bite of sharp teeth sinking into his bottom lip.

"Oww," he cried in mock pain.

She laughed and pushed away from him. He followed and, when she rolled from a slow crawl to her back to float, their fingers brushed, then merged and they floated on the bobbing current, looking at the dusky sky above them. Clay knew he'd never felt more at peace or in tune with another person in his life.

"Clay?" she whispered long moments later.

"Hhhhmmm," he answered.

"We'd better go back ashore."

"Okay. I guess we're both starting to turn into prunes," he said.

Neither made the first move to turn around for a few more heartbeats. Without thought, they turned as one. When their feet touched the rocky bottom of the lake and water ran off them, he turned her completely into his arms.

Their kiss was warm, moving to hot in a slow, languid fashion familiar to him. He had always been a slow and easy kind of guy, especially after he'd taken the edge off as they had earlier. It was one reason he'd rarely stayed in a relationship for very long before. Once he'd had a woman, he lost some interest, not only physically but mentally as well.

But with Edith he found that, although the petting and playing was wonderful, his body wasn't content to just stop there. Kissing in the surf was fine for a while, but soon he'd need to take her.

He tried to concentrate on the taste and feel of her rather than the growing urge to be deep inside her again. She tasted, not of lilacs but of honey, not the sickening sweetness of processed honey, but with a wild, fruity taste fresh from the hive. Clay didn't have a solid memory of eating honey that fresh, but he was as certain of the taste as he was that Wall Street was in Manhattan.

She wrapped her arms around his neck and rested her body against his. Although he was a good eight inches taller than her, he didn't mind bending down to meet her halfway. Her breasts were full and heavy, but the way they pushed against his chest, her soft skin rubbing against his hair was exquisitely pleasurable. He kept one arm firmly around her waist, lifting her feet off the rocky bottom, but his free hand took pleasure in cupping one of her breasts, rubbing the satiny underside and turning circles around her firming nipple. He promised himself he would taste that little bud of flesh again before he was done. But there was no hurry. They had all night.

She moaned a little and it was a sound that sent a flutter of need arcing across his skin and into his blood. Still he lingered on savoring the feel, taste and scent of her, this woman who was already becoming a huge part of his soul.

But the growing desire couldn't be ignored. His faithful Samson was already making that fact well known, having risen to his full height and demanding attention.

He put his hands under the globes of her wonderful ass and lifted her. He was going to take her here and now, where they stood.

"No," she said as she placed a hand on his chest. "Let me do this."

He hesitated and then lowered her back to the shore. Edith knelt and looked up at him. The smile of desire and warmth nearly made him take a step back. But her cool hands tracing down the length of his cock and balls made him shiver and his feet were glued in place.

"So much strength and beauty here," she said, the breath of her words blowing over him. Samson nearly shivered in response. "I'm going to sculpt this part of you in onyx."

Clay wanted to laugh at the absurdity of that, but he lost all ability to speak when he felt her tongue swirl over his tip.

"Yum. Cool, but so hard," she hummed against him. "Wonder how long it will take to heat him up."

Slowly, like she was inhaling an ice cream cone, she worked her way around his tip. She licked in circles around his crown and front to back across his slit, which was wet with the mixture of his desire, her saliva and the water from the Niagara.

He thought he would nearly go blind with desire when she continued to work just the tip of him with exquisite gentleness.

"God, Edith," he groaned. His lower body was thrusting forward, but she wasn't taking the hint.

She squeezed gently, but with enough force to get his attention.

"You have to relax and give me control," she said. "That's the bet, remember?"

He did remember and he should be able to do it. He knew no matter who took the lead, he was going to come out the winner in this game.

As if she could read his mind she spoke. "You know, it doesn't all have to be about control. It can be much simpler."

He frowned. He sensed she wasn't just talking about sex.

"I'm not very good at relinquishing control," he said.

"Believe me, I know. Don't you think it's time you trusted someone else enough to try?"

Clay pulled away. At first he didn't think she was going to let him go, but she did. He started to turn away from her, then turned back to help her up. When she ignored his outstretched hand, he laughed.

"You're a good one to talk about relinquishing control. You wouldn't even take my help standing up."

"I didn't need your help," she retorted. She walked back to the shore and then headed back the way they came.

"This entire ridiculous thing started because you're too stubborn to take help—even if it's the best thing for you," he said. He didn't know where this was coming from, but it was if he couldn't keep it inside anymore. "Good God woman, I want to make you famous. What the hell is wrong with you?"

"What's wrong with me? What's wrong with me?" her voice was rising.

Now they were back behind her house. He could see the potter's wheel, the clay that she had started working her magic on. It was going to be magnificent when it was finished. It was almost there now.

"I'm not the one who is burned out and on the verge of a breakdown before he's fifty. I'm not the one who is so set on being famous he's forgotten what it means to be happy."

"I'm happy," he protested. For a fleeting second something she'd said niggled at his brain, but his rising anger wiped it away. "I'm so damn happy I'm about to burst. Who the hell wouldn't be happy being me? I own everything I've ever wanted. I'm one of the richest men in the world. I'm a role model."

"But does it make you happy? Do even know what that's like anymore? Do you even remember what it feels like? Do you remember how you felt in that gallery in SoHo in 1991?"

Clay stopped and stared. "What do you know about SoHo?"

"I know everything, Clay. Everything. I'm the woman you crushed to buy your first gallery."

*   *   *

Edith rubbed her hands up and down her arms trying to erase the coldness that seemed to be sinking into her bones despite the long-sleeve tee she wore.

She had the world's worst timing. She had all her life…what had made her think this was going to be different?

Cruel and clueless, that's what I am, she thought.

How could I just blurt it out without preparing him more? And why did I pick that moment to do it? I should've waited until the weekend was over. He'd have been more receptive then.

Edith walked over to where her prize was stashed and pulled it up on the easel. It was perfect, absolutely perfect. She wasn't going to ignore it.

She'd do whatever it took, take as long as needed, to find him. When she did, she'd make everything right.

CHAPTER 3

Clay slammed the cell phone shut and paced across the hotel room. Niagara Falls was forty stories below, but he didn't see the majestic beauty of the landmark. He was thinking about the woman he'd left behind in Youngstown and the information his secretary had just faxed him.

Everything she'd said was true. Edith Agnes Raines had been one of the top contenders for the gallery in SoHo. He remembered now there'd been something about a verbal agreement between the owner and someone. Of course, at the time, he'd shrugged that away as inconsequential. He'd learned early in life that money talks and words walk. Apparently, Edith hadn't learned that hard fact of life until he taught her.

Clay rubbed a hand over his chest. There was something lingering there. He knew the pain wasn't physical. He had bungled everything so much he was uncertain what to do next. The safest bet was the easiest play. He should walk away and forget he'd ever met Edith Raines. He should forget all about her talent and move forward. There would be other artists, other talents to bring to the world.

Clay flipped the phone open. He was punching out the number his secretary had included in the information she'd faxed to him without even thinking. It would be easy to say what he wanted to say without looking at her face, seeing again the disappointment that had been there when he'd beat a retreat like a scared kid.

He closed the phone before the first ring. What could he say? That she was right? That he hadn't been happy in so long he didn't remember what happy was? That he knew money didn't buy everything?

Damn it, no. He wasn't going to second guess his life. Not now. He was extremely good at what he did. So what if sometimes his palms itched with the urge to pick up a brush and take it to a canvas? That was for artists. Not for him. He wasn't an artist. He was an art dealer.

There was a knock at the door of his room. He was tempted to ignore it. It was probably either housekeeping or another fax from his secretary. Either way he wasn't up to dealing with minutia now. When the knock sounded again, he rolled his eyes, walked across the room and opened the door.

"Whatever it is, can it wait a..." He stopped speaking when he realized Edith stood in the hall. "It's you."

"Yes. Sorry to bother you but I—"

"You're not bothering me," Clay interrupted in a rush. He held the door open wider and resisted the urge to grab her by the arm and haul her into his room. "Come in. I was just calling you."

"Oh?" Edith smiled.

Clay's heart beat triple time. She'd smiled at him like that once or twice before. Both times the results had been spectacular.

"Well, I was thinking about it," he clarified.

She nodded and looked around his room. "Nice place."

"It's okay. I was kind of growing used to your place in the woods, though." He shut the door and followed her across the living area of his suite.

When she stood in front of the window and looked down at the rapids rushing to the summit, he had to bunch his hands in his pockets to keep from grabbing her and dragging her into his bed.

"I know it wasn't your normal style," she said. "It's home to me."

"Yes, I finally figured that out." He paused. He was groping and he didn't like it. He wanted to put everything right, but was unsure of where he stood. If it was just business, he could have followed a normal game plan. This was much more than business. He wanted to say what was in his heart, but once again he felt his courage desert him.

"Is that why you don't want to sign with my gallery? Because you're afraid to leave home?" he asked.

Edith laughed. "No. Although you have to admit my last experience with a national gallery fell somewhat short."

Clay almost breathed a sigh of relief. At least they were focusing on something he could deal with. "Why do you say that? Just because you got caught between two immovable forces fighting for a prime piece of property doesn't mean you weren't qualified. If we hadn't been so intent on getting the gallery, the stakes wouldn't have been so high."

Edith looked at him curiously. "Do really believe the only reason I won't sign with you is because you stole my gallery from me?"

"I didn't steal it. I bought it for seventy percent above market value at the time. That's how business is done," Clay retorted.

"By you," she replied.

"By everyone. Look, it was a long time ago, but obviously you've found your niche. Believe me…someone with your talent wouldn't have been happy selling other people's work. Your talent should be the one showcased."

Edith nodded. "I know that now. What about your talent?"

He ran a hand through his hair in exasperation. "Woman, what are you talking about? My talent is showcased. That's why my name is on the door in fifty galleries worldwide."

Edith frowned and shook her head. Then she walked over to the door and pulled a large portfolio forward. She must have set it against the wall when she came in the room because he hadn't noticed it, so intent was he on just seeing her again.

"I found a painting ten years ago. It was going to be the cornerstone of my gallery when I took it over. It's by an unknown artist. Would you like to see it?"

Clay sighed. "What I really want to do is talk about us. You and me. But I'll look at your discovery if I must."

Edith slowly lifted the picture from the leather carrier. "I think you'll be glad you did. This particular piece is rich in texture and shows an intensity unusual in a young artist."

Clay almost laughed. She was mimicking his gallery manager in SoHo perfectly. But when he saw the first touch of color on the painting, he lost all his ability to speak.

"Recognize this?" she asked softly. "You should. You painted it. I discovered it hidden in a workroom at the back of the SoHo gallery. I was going to find you and make you a star. But you never gave me the chance."

"I destroyed that painting. No one was ever to see it again," Clay finally said.

"Why? Why would you destroy something so beautiful? So stirring? So perfect?"

"Because that isn't good enough to pay the freight," Clay said. "I know. I'm an expert at looking at something and immediately predicting if it'll be valuable one day. I have customers who depend on it."

Edith nodded. "I never thought you blind, but I can tell you are when it comes to your own worth at least because I look at this painting and see something of great value."

Duncan snorted. "Value? It has no value. Even the most novice eye can tell the technique is unpolished, the artistic value is nil and the subject matter has as much creativity as a five-year-old would find in a coloring book."

Edith glared at him. "Now I know you're blind. Look at this!" She brought it to the windows where the sun was shining through the sparkling glass. "This was done by someone with a huge well of talent. Even if it isn't worth a ton of money in the modern art world, it has sentimental value. This is your home. This is how you saw it. How can turn your back on this? All this time I was under the impression you're an art lover, but you're an art hater. You love money."

"You don't know anything. You don't know what my life is like." Clay felt as if she was ripping his skin off inch by inch. His only choice was to hide his pain in anger.

"I know that this"—Edith raged as she held the painting up in his face—"is a gift from God. You do not turn your back on it. You can't."

"A gift from God? More like a gift from Satan." Clay sneered. "Let me tell you about gifts. Gifts don't pay the bills. Gifts don't put food in the bellies of children or parents who desperately need help to live."

"Is everything about money for you?"

"Listen to who's talking. You're a society girl who was a flop at the only real job she's ever had and ran to the middle of nowhere to drop out and hide."

"I didn't come here to hide. I came here because I realized I, too, have a gift from God and it's not something I can turn my back on. I came here because I don't have to have fame and money as long as I have my art. Can you say the same?"

"There's the pot again," Clay said. "Have you ever known what it's truly like to be needy? Have you ever gone to bed so hungry you think the pain is going to gnaw a hole through your stomach into your spine?"

"No. Have you?"

"Yes. But that isn't the worst of it. The worst is watching someone you love, someone you've sworn to take care of, die a slow, agonizing death because your gift from God is as worthless as a handful of spit."

Edith looked solemnly at him for a moment. "I see. Who was she?"

"It doesn't matter," he began. When she looked at him, he sighed. "It was my mother. She wouldn't hear of me getting a "real" job because she was so sure I was going to be the next great artist of my time. While I was working on this painting, she starved to death."

* * *

There were a few seconds of silence. One moment Clay was wishing he could take back his hurled words; the next he was in Edith's arms, her warmth and sweet lilac and honey smell wrapped around him.

He lifted her up and she put her legs around his waist and wound her arms tightly around his neck. He was crying into her neck. He felt weak and ashamed. She started murmuring to him. Senseless words, soothing words, healing words.

She told him she was sorry for the death of his mother, for the loss of his innocence, for the way she'd forced him to tell her everything. Then she told him that everything would be okay. Things would be right again for him.

Somewhere, as the minutes merged into hours, his wounds were purged. Her words became gentle kisses that he needed like the food his mother had been denied.

The kisses soon became deeper and more intense. He needed these even more than the gentle ones.

They moved with silent agreement to the bed and she undressed him slowly. Her hands moved over his face, down his neck to his shoulders and chest. When she allowed her tongue to play with his nipples, licking and nipping, Clay lost it. He had to have her now. It had been way too long and he couldn't stand it another moment.

He tore off her clothes, uncaring when, in his haste and need, her panties split across the seam of the crotch opening her to him. He knew he should take more time, to make sure she was as aroused and as ready for his penetration as he was. But he couldn't control himself. He had to be inside her. He thrust forward and, though she wasn't completely dry, she was a long way from lubricated. But his eyes closed in relief when her muscles relaxed and allowed his full penetration.

Her thatch hair mingled with his own and he could feel his tip nudging against her cervix and knew he had returned home.

She was on top, her legs bent at the knees and resting on each side of his hips.

The position allowed for the deepest penetration and he felt each caress of her inner muscles against his hard shaft as she adjusted to his size. He was able, with the last shred of his control, to keep from thrusting repeatedly as his body was craving. His vision grayed as need battled with desire to make some part of this good for her.

She leaned forward and placed her hands on his chest, then nipped his chin with her teeth.

"Don't hold back," she said. "Give me everything."

He closed his eyes as the roar of desire poured through his blood. Her words loosed his chain of control.

He pistoned his hips once, twice, three times and then lost himself as his climax rushed from him.

Moving as if his arms and legs were weighted after his violent climax, he reached up with his hand and tweaked her nipples. He thumbed them up and down, then palmed each in turn. Edith bit down on her bottom lip and began moving in a slow, erotic dance, rising up and down on his shaft.

His juices made the movement easier and he felt himself starting to harden again.

"God, I can't believe what you do to me," he moaned. "I feel like a kid again."

Edith grinned down at him and then reached with her own hands, covering his as they massaged her breasts. "Well, that's a good thing because I need you to be young again."

She did something, flexed her inner muscles and it was as if someone had sent a jolt of desire to his cock. He hardened fully once more and felt each rasp of her muscles tighten around him.

"God, I'm hard again," he grunted. He tried to focus on the half-moon birthmark above her right breast to keep his vision from graying. It wasn't really successful because it seemed to just edge him closer to insanity.

"That's it," she said, leaning forward, her nipple within reach of his mouth. His tongue slipped out and covered the nipple and their still-joined fingers as his body embraced each new feeling.

"Ooh, yes," she groaned.

His pelvis started thrusting again and she met each thrust in a sensual ride that took them both to heaven. They reached the summit together and their shouts of release rocked around the room.

When he came back to earth, he felt lighter and happier than he had in decades. He opened his eyes and smiled at the woman responsible for it all.

She smiled back. "Well, I guess I'd better get going," she said slowly disengaging her arms and legs from him.

"Where?" he asked, resisting the urge to keep her locked against him.

"Well, if I'm going to have a big showing in a major world-wide gallery, I'd better get busy," she replied.

"Wait a minute!" He grabbed her hand as she moved off the bed. "I didn't win the bet...you did."

She looked at him. "Well, actually, I'd say we both won. But that isn't why I'm going to sign with you."

"Why are you?"

"Are you taking the offer back?"

They spoke simultaneously.

"No," Clay said. "I want you in the gallery, but I don't want you there unless it's something you've seen for yourself. As far as I'm concerned, if you want to continue to just sculpt and sell it yourself in your store, that's fine with me."

Edith smiled. "So you finally understand for me it isn't about the fame and fortune?"

"Yes," Clay said. "I don't really understand why you would turn it down when it comes, but I do understand it doesn't have to be about the money."

"Good. I understand when you stopped painting, it had to be about the money for you at that time," Edith said.

Clay smiled. "Thank you. But you know you were right about one thing. I have always wondered 'what if.'"

Edith turned her head to one side. "What if?"

"Yeah. What if I hadn't believed the one art teacher who told me I'd never be successful and tried to place my work in a gallery. What if I hadn't let one bad review make me stop?"

"You stopped because an art teacher told you your work was bad?" Edith sounded amazed.

"Well, yeah. I don't know if you've ever experienced it, but it's not a very pleasant thing to deal with."

Edith laughed. "Oh, I know. It's a lot like having an accountant telling you you lost everything on a risky gamble to buy a gallery."

Clay smiled. "I guess it is." He took her hand in his and linked their fingers. "Where does that leave us?" he asked.

Edith looked down at their hands together. "I honestly don't know, Clay. I don't know if I can go back to living full-time in New York."

"I don't have to live there," he said quickly.

"No, but you can't live here," she answered. "I know it. You do, too. Be honest... you'd go crazy if you had to stay here for even one winter."

Clay sighed. "Well, that's probably true, but does everything have to be so black and white for you? Can't we compromise?"

Edith smiled slowly. "I've never been very good at compromise."

"Neither have I. Maybe it'll be easier if we both give just a little," he said.

Edith paused as if she had to truly consider it. "Okay. But just so you know, I'm going to have my lawyer look over the contract you want me to sign."

He grinned. It was one showing a lot of white, sharp teeth, like the predator he was. "I wouldn't expect less."

"And my accountant."

"Oh, God, we may never get the deal signed then."

"Well, you'll just have to work real hard at making it worth my while to skip over a few of the details."

She hooked her legs around his waist and he hefted her up closer to him by cupping her ass.

"I thought you didn't care for fame and fortune." His attempt at serious distress was lost when he nibbled lightly on her lips.

She sighed at the feeling of coming home. "I don't. But I also don't like being poor."

Clay laughed. "I think I'm finally getting it. All this was nothing more than a set-up, wasn't it?"

Edith tried to pretend innocence while she was working her fingers over the firm muscles of his chest, down his rock hard abs to the spot where Samson was already stirring to massive life.

"Me? Try to set up the great, wonderful Clay Fife? Never?"

His laugh ended on a strangled groan when she shifted and slid over him, taking him like a mare meeting a stallion.

"God, what have I gotten into?"

EPILOGUE

12 months later

"Are you sure you want to go to this thing? I know it really isn't your scene." Clay stood nervously at their bedroom door. He was tugging on the tie of his tux as if he'd never worn one.

Edith looked over at him and smiled as her heart swelled. He was such a gorgeous man and he was all hers. Dressed like now in a black tux with an impossibly white shirt and onyx studs at his wrists, he could have stepped off the glossy pages of a Fortune 500 magazine cover. He was just as handsome when he was dressed down in comfortable jeans or even better when he was posing nude for her.

He'd quickly gotten over his shyness at posing for her and they had spent many pleasurable afternoons together—sometimes at her complex in Youngstown; sometimes at his homes in Milan and New York.

"You've got to be nuts if you think I'm going to let a little queasiness keep me from this opening," she said. "Even if I am as big as a whale."

"I don't see any whales here, just a beautiful, sexy wife who is protecting our daughter right now," Clay replied, laying his hand on her full belly.

"You know you'd better get used to the fact this could be a boy," she teased.

"No way," Clay said. "It's going to be a girl. I can guarantee it. But if you'd like, we can stay home tonight and you can try to convince me."

Edith laughed. "Not a chance, buster. We have an opening to attend. You shouldn't be nervous, you know."

"Easy for you to say. You're the toast of the entire art world. Just like I predicted." Clay ran his hand over his collar as he led her down to the waiting limo. "You sure this looks okay?"

"Absolutely. But you can always go wearing our favorite towel if you'd rather. That would certainly stir up some interest."

"You've got to be kidding. I'd never live that down. As it is, I had to turn down the sheik again yesterday on the onyx."

"Do tell. What was his offer this time?"

"Twenty million?"

"Dollars?"

Clay just looked at Edith. "Of course, dollars."

"Hhhm. Maybe I'd better talk to the sheik tonight."

"Maybe you'd better not," Clay replied. "I will not be explaining to little Agnes when she arrives why her daddy let her mother sculpt him that way and then sold it to the highest bidder."

"We'll see," Edith said as their limo pulled up to the gallery.

Clay helped her out of the car and she stood looking up at the discreet but easily read sign above the door that read, "Scotland Through My Eyes, by Clay Fife."

"Oh look darling, it's great! I'm so proud of you!"

She looked over at the man of her heart and smiled. "I knew you'd be a big hit. I just knew it!"

THE COMING

———————————

On a grassy knoll overlooking a Lake Erie shoal waits a fair maid.

Every day she looks out her high window to the west, to the south, to the north, hoping to see her true love's ship coming to take her away.

Weeks, months and years pass with no sight of his ship on the horizon. Believing he would never purposely leave her to her landlocked prison, she makes a vow to never rest until they can be together again. She will walk the halls of this place for eternity until reunited with her true love.

CHAPTER 1

Luke St. Clair thrust shaking legs out from under the sheet and put his feet on the cold hardwood floor of the bedroom. He ran a hand over his face, wiping away the sweat lingering there.

He had to be going bonkers. It was the only explanation for seeing ghosts.

Hell, seeing ghosts would be a snap. What he was experiencing every time he closed his eyes was much worse.

He was having sex with ghosts.

The evidence of the latest encounter was pooled against his stomach and running down his groin. Disgusted, he got up and strode into the bathroom. As he waited for the water to heat, then stepped inside the stall, he knew he had to do something about this situation.

As he soaped and rinsed away the evidence of the latest visit, he wondered what the hell was wrong with him. He'd lived in this old house on the Lake Erie shoreline near Buffalo, New York for just over a week. The house itself was a wreck. But he had plans for it.

A nineteenth century Victorian that had fallen on hard times, it was the perfect place for him to try all the new, environment friendly and computer-assisted building techniques he specialized in.

This was the project that was going to send him to the next level of contracting. Soon, he'd have clients nationwide. Heck, if a few things fell into place, he'd have clients worldwide.

The key was this house. He looked around what was currently the house's only bathroom, in its various stages of disrepair. The walls were stripped bare so he could see the new pipes to the solar-powered water heater he'd just installed yesterday. It was a costly addition, but he wanted to make this house completely self-sufficient again, as it had been in the 1800s, but with all the conveniences of a twenty-first-century home. He'd be adding a back-up, traditional gas-powered system this week, but he hoped he could go ahead and start re-plastering and tiling this room this afternoon.

He had such plans for this room and the master bedroom next to it. He was using only the finest materials. Real cherry-wood for the trim and baseboards in the bedroom to go with the cherry hardwood floor he had ordered. He'd bring in modern conveniences like a glassed walled shower, spa tub and Italian tile on the floor.

It would have the look and feel of a grand bathroom of the 1890s, with all the conveniences and plush accessories available today. But Luke didn't just plan to make this house a replica of a Victorian mansion. There were probably a couple dozen guys right in western New York who could do that today. His differences, that were going to push the house over the top, were mechanical. He'd already installed the exterior solar panels on the roof. They were the type that looked like regular steel roof shingles from the ground but, from the air, their solar capabilities were revealed.

In addition to heating the water, the solar panels would also provide some of the electricity. His plans also called for a windmill to be located about a hundred yards from the house. If all went well, he could see the future owners never having to use either traditional electric or gas power.

Most had scoffed at his idea. How would it work here on the eastern shoreline of Lake Erie known more for its snow than its sun? His ace in the hole was providing the backup wind system.

In addition to designing the plans, Luke was determined to do most of the wiring and finishing construction himself. He'd have work crews in to help with the big jobs—like the crew coming this afternoon to drywall—and some of the basic construction, but the rest he would handle himself. Still, it was a huge undertaking, even for someone with his construction and design experience.

This was the first time he'd attempted something so complete on his own. In the week he'd been here, he'd worked like a dog from sun-up to sundown. He was proud of his progress. But he was also extremely tired.

Which made these nighttime escapades more frustrating. He was so tired at night he literally fell into bed. But every night, he'd be awakened from a deep sleep by a sound. At first he'd thought he wasn't awake. He was just dreaming.

But the feel of hands stroking down his chest, of lips and tongue surrounding his cock was not a dream.

Nor was the ghostly apparition that had moved over him, encasing his responsive rod inside her body.

Luke felt his body hardening just at the memory. No, there was no other explanation for it. He had to be crazy. If so, it was a helluva way to go.

Because, on this seventh morning, he found himself wanting not to work on this house, but to fall back asleep and not wake until his ghostly lover reappeared.

Instead, he dressed quickly and went downstairs to the kitchen. He cursed slightly when he saw the clock on the kitchen wall. It was later than he thought. He had an inspector coming at eight this morning. It was five to now. Thanks to the automated coffee maker, he'd have time for a cup of coffee to at least shake some of the cobwebs loose. He grabbed the handle of the glass carafe, tempted to drink the brew straight out of it. Thoughts of burning his mouth had him grabbing hurriedly for the mug from yesterday and pouring fresh liquid in it, then drinking it down. It still burned his mouth, but at least he didn't spill it on his shirt as he probably would have drinking it straight from the pot.

Today's inspection was crucial to his plans. If they okayed the plumbing lines he'd installed, along with the rough-ins for the solar system, he could drywall and paint the walls. He could also drop the electrical and plumbing lines for the other two bathrooms he planned the house to have and then get to work on putting in the new wiring throughout the first floor.

In addition to this house having the most energy efficient heating and water systems, he also planned for it to be completely wired for any and all technology with wireless access on every floor and built-in surround-sound speakers. Every household system would be controlled by a mainframe computer in the basement.

Luke rolled open the electronic schematics across his makeshift table—a sheet of wallboard stretched across three sawhorses—and looked things over again. He believed he'd worked out all the problems and now all he had to do was file these plans with the county offices, get their tentative approval and then start running the wires.

A loud knock sounded on the front door and pulled him away from his work.

"Good, he's here," Luke muttered. He walked out of the nearly gutted kitchen, through a dark hall, past the dining room, which had holes in the ceiling, and a front parlor that shared a huge fireplace only an inch from falling down with the dining room, and swung open the heavy front door.

The woman was tiny, probably no more than five feet in stocking feet and wore baby-sized work boots on her feet. Her short legs were encased in jeans wrapping around a nicely curved ass. His palms itched with the desire to cup those perfect globes and squeeze. He felt himself hardening and tore his gaze from her lower body as she twisted back from looking at the lake to him standing in the doorway.

He took in the rest of her. Her ash blonde hair was tied up in one of those interwoven ponytails. What did they call them? French braids? That was it. He knew of some French things he would like to do to her, but braiding wasn't one of them. Her blue eyes were lively and interesting, like a cool dip in a deep pool. She wore a T-shirt that fit over her ample bosom like she was ready to enter a bar-room contest.

Stupendous ass and wondrous tits, he thought. Had he died in his sleep after all?

"You St. Clair?" Her voice was husky, like she'd been just wakened from a night of rocking hard sex.

Suddenly, Luke knew he wanted to be the man to rock into her tonight.

Her eyes narrowed and she cleared her throat. Luke felt the embarrassment climb across his neck to his face.

"Yeah, I'm St. Clair," he stuttered. He knew there was no hiding the evidence of his desire that had swelled inside his work jeans.

"I'm your inspector."

"Oh, yeah, right. I've been expecting you." He stood to the side to allow her to come in. "Can I get you some coffee or something?"

He hoped the offer would help with his inspection and give him a few moments to get thoughts of ravaging her off his mind.

"Sure," she answered. She walked agilely up the plank he'd lain across what had once been a front porch and into his house. He noticed she looked around with some interest. "I'm Pam Lukasiac."

He smiled at her over his shoulder. "Hello, Pam. Let me get you a mug and then I'll show you around."

"So you're the new owner. I understand you've got some big plans for it."

He handed her a steaming mug of coffee and indicated the small packets of sweetener and creamer he had stashed in a styrofoam cup.

"Black is fine," Pam said. "This place has a lot of history, you know."

Luke swallowed his mouthful of coffee and nodded. Talking about mundane stuff was helping to get his mind off the testosterone still raging through his bloodstream. "I know some of it but haven't had a lot of time to really dig deep."

Pam looked down. Luke thought he saw a flare of unholy glee before it vanished. He wondered what that was about.

"I'm sure if you contact the Erie County Historical Society they can give you all the information," she said with a smile.

"Oh, come on…you look like you've got the information. Are you really going to keep it a secret and make me call the historical society?" Luke asked.

Her eyes met his and he clearly saw the gleam of amusement there. "Well, this was a…some would call it…a hotel, of sorts," she said.

"A hotel?" Luke was stumped. He hadn't seen anything about a hotel being here. "Here? But it's so far from downtown. Do you mean it was a resort?"

He could believe that. The house sat on top of a gently sloping knoll, and the sandy beachfront at the bottom would make a good place for bathing. There was a shoal about fifty yards from the shore and he imagined it would have provided a nice little calm inlet for families to play. But the biggest draw to the house, and the reason he was set to turn it into a single-family home now, was the unending views of Lake Erie visible from every front room. Yes, he could see it as a perfect family vacation spot for the wealthy 1890s family.

Pam bit her bottom lip, drawing his gaze to her mouth. Her mouth was shaped like a bow. Her lips were full and rosy red. He had a sudden vivid picture of those lips stretched wide to wrap around his…

"Resort is one word for it. Brothel, though, would be more accurate."

Brothel? Luke nearly groaned. "Ah." He had to clear his throat twice to get his words to come out.

Pam laughed. The sound stroked his flaming body like a warm caress.

"I'm sorry. I'm really sorry. I shouldn't have told you like that. I just couldn't resist when you thought it was a resort. It was just too funny."

Luke shook his head. "No…I guess I walked right into that, didn't I? Not that it matters. I just didn't expect a brothel to be out in the middle of nowhere. I could almost understand it now, but a hundred years ago, this was a long way for the lonely men from the city to come just to get laid."

Pam nodded. "Yes, it was. But this place didn't cater to the citizens of Buffalo. Its clientele were the sailors on the merchant ships as they traveled on Lake Erie."

Luke watched as she talked. Her features were animated, her blue eyes sparkling. He shouldn't be so attracted to her. She wasn't the type of woman he was normally drawn to. In fact, she exuded home and hearth earthiness. Never mind that she was a building inspector—a job once limited to ex-contractors. He'd seen more and more women doing it in the last few years. No…what attracted him wasn't her job, though it seemed to fit her like a glove. It was the roundness that normally would have sent him running as fast as he could. He liked his women to have hard bodies and sharp minds. He wanted them focused on fast sex and no ties.

This woman looked like she could have been the model for Eve, the mother of all women. Worse, thinking about the history of this house, he could see this woman servicing him for the rest of…

"Some have even claimed this house is haunted."

Her words snapped him from his introspection.

"Haunted?"

She laughed. It was that low, sexy one again. Luke really didn't need that laugh to get him going, but it did nonetheless.

"Yes. Haunted. They say the prostitutes move through the halls at night and any unescorted man gets special treatment." She paused then frowned. "They also say there's one woman in particular. She's waiting for her true love to return."

"Wow," he said. He felt like there were fingers running down his spine and resisted the urge to look over his shoulder. He didn't want to know if his ghost lady was forming even as they spoke.

"So, Mr. St. Clair, had any strange visitors at night?" she asked looking over her shoulder at him.

"Actually, yes. I think I have."

*   *   *

Pam didn't know how to respond to his bombshell. She had been teasing in an attempt to keep him from seeing what an effect he had on her. When he'd opened the door earlier, she had felt like someone had punched her directly in the solar plexis.

He was the man who'd been haunting her dreams every night for the last month.

The last one had happened earlier this morning. She didn't have to close her eyes to remember the way it had felt as if real hands were stroking across her breasts, down her stomach until reaching her aching mons. The edge of desire had hovered desperately just outside her reach. Was it any wonder that she was one big aching mass of nerves? Was it also any wonder that just standing here with this man who was a stranger, yet so familiar, would set those nerves to riot levels again?

As she stared at the blueprints she needed to approve, she tried to dissect his looks. Maybe then they wouldn't make her clit swell every time his gaze passed over her, even impersonally.

He was tall and muscular. Wearing jeans and a stark white tee like now, she could see the outline of his strong pecs, shoulders and flat stomach. In her dreams, he'd been tanned. Gazing at the deep, dark skin covering the ropy muscles of his arms, she could see the reality now. This tan wasn't some namby-pamby salon one. It was the kind burned into skin from a hot western or southern sun. His long hair was reddish-brown and more than a little wild. Now, he was wearing it bound by a simple piece of leather in a neat little bob at his neck. His eyes were brown, like doe eyes, which seemed to be able to read all the way to her soul.

As he talked about his plans for the house and what he wanted to do, they were drawing hers like magnets. All in all he was one mouth-watering package.

Too bad he was obviously a nut-case because the last thing she needed was some flaky California type who thought he saw the ghosts of Knob Hill racing about the halls of the house he was renovating. She didn't want to examine the fact she could be the kettle calling the pot black since she was either crazy or believed in ghosts as well.

Not that I need or want any kind of man, Pam thought. Even one who looked like a god and smiled like a dream. *Those lips of his are another problem,* she thought. They were full without being fat. She licked her own wanting, with an almost impossible desire, to bite into his lips and see if they tasted of sin like they looked.

Then there were his eyes to consider. They were normal in every way except the color.

One minute they were just a normal brown, a color so common it would be easy to overlook, except she kept thinking she was sinking into them, that she was about to be swallowed whole by them.

Then those completely normal brown eyes turned to a warm hazel that made her think of cozy fires and languid sex. She looked again and tried not to think about the sex part.

"So what do you think?" His voice finally broke through her thoughts.

Pam realized he wanted her opinion. The problem was she had been so intent on thinking about him, she hadn't been listening to what he was saying.

"I'm sorry," she stammered.

His smile was slow and devastatingly sexy.

He was standing close to her. Way closer than she should allow. She could feel the heat from his body brushing near hers and her response was immediate.

"I asked if you could find any problems with my plans?" His words were ordinary, businesslike. They were not in any way suggestive.

So why was her clit swelling, and her nipples hardening? She couldn't seem to force herself to look away from the mesmerizing, seductive look in those gorgeous eyes, or from the hypnotic way his lips moved as he spoke the normal words.

She had a sudden flashback to her dream early this morning. It had been his lips moving down her breasts, his tongue flicking between them for a taste before he suckled her deep inside her mouth.

Oh God, she was about to come right here, right this moment while standing fully dressed talking to a client. She pulled herself back from the edge with a start.

"Your plans look fine," she said.

He laughed softly and Pam felt the sound stroll down her spine like hot fingers.

"Excellent. Truly excellent," he said. "Would you like to begin the inspection with the wiring or the plumbing?"

Well, at least one of them was able to concentrate on what they were supposed to be doing.

"I think…let's take a look at the plumbing upstairs, then work our way downstairs where we can take care of the plumbing and heating at once. Has the gas company already been out here to check the system and check on the lines?"

"No. They're coming later this week. I want to make sure the solar and wind systems are really carrying the main utilities weight. The gas is merely a backup, so as long as it's just me here, I figured if there are any glitches, it won't matter if the gas isn't hooked up immediately."

Pam frowned as she followed him down the hall and up the stairs to the third floor.

"You sound like you think renewable energy is going to completely power this house."

"That's my plan," he answered.

"I know solar energy has been effective in the south and out west, but they haven't really proven it here."

"Ah, but that's why I'm installing the windmill next. That's going to pick up where the solar drops off."

"Hhmm," Pam replied.

They had reached the bathroom. She could see and smell the lingering evidence of his morning bath, an evergreen-scented soap, damp wash cloth and towel hanging neatly over the edge of an ancient claw-footed tub with a plain white plastic shower liner attached to a cheap metal rod.

She had to pull her mind forcefully away from the clear picture she saw of his tall, lean, naked body standing under the hot, pulsing spray. She clenched her fingers into her palms, making a fist to keep from touching his clothed chest now. Taking a deep breath…no…that was a mistake because it filled her nostrils with the clean scent of him again. She walked over to check out where the pipes were visible between the studs.

She felt him move behind her and felt the lance of desire race down her spine.

"You doing all the plumbing yourself?" Surely he wouldn't realize her breathlessness was from desire.

"Yes," he answered.

He was close to her, but not close enough to touch. So why was she certain she felt his fingers brush along her arm? The shiver of desire was as hot as a shock of electricity and zinged through her central nervous system straight into her core. She actually thought her pussy lips were quivering with excitement. She looked quickly over her shoulder to make sure he wasn't touching her. Big mistake. The desire she saw in his eyes was like looking at hazel fire. She had to get away or be burned at the stake.

She knelt and inspected the plumbing. "Well, this looks good. I don't see any problems so far."

She felt his nearness when he got down to her level, his legs spread in a squat. It was if she had sonar or eyes in the back of her head where he was concerned. Every move he made telegraphed itself to her. Instead of moving away, or making sure she was out of harm's way, all the warning did was entice her like a weird form of foreplay.

When he reached across her to point to one of the pipe joints, she felt as if she was completely surrounded by his heat. His fresh scent teased her nose and her mouth opened. For a moment, she felt like Skittles, her cat, and wished she could simply climb onto his lap and burrow in for a long nap. She would knead his bulge with sharp, little claws, padding and stroking...

When she realized she was staring at the way his lips moved as if caressing each word he spoke, Pam blinked. What had he just said?

"Are you all right?" he asked.

She nodded. She had to get out of here. The scents of him and well, something else about being on this floor was affecting her in a way she didn't need.

"I don't see any problems here, Mr. St. Clair. Let's take a look in the basement."

She started to move and felt a wave of dizziness wash over her. She felt like she was falling. To catch herself, she put her hand out. It landed on his hard thigh.

He grabbed her arms and pulled her against him. He was being noble, that's all, Pam told herself. But when she looked up, his eyes were saying much more than nobility. Without thought, she lifted her lips to his. Their kiss started slowly, a tentative meeting between two strangers.

It was also the most erotic thing Pam had ever experienced. As she had wondered earlier, she now discovered his lips were full without being soft. She luxuriated in them, relishing the way they moved across and over her own.

As her tongue traced the outline of first the top lip, with its slight nick at the pinnacle, then over to the point it joined with his bottom lip, all she thought about was getting more, tasting more.

Down she went onto his bottom lip. She suckled a little and his lips parted, allowing her tongue entry inside his mouth. She could taste the remnants of his coffee here. It was dark, like a finely-brewed espresso, but more head-spinning to her than any coffee she'd ever had. She caught her breath at the way the taste rocketed through her. His tongue met hers and they shared an intimate dance.

Parry. Thurst.

Relax.

Dart back past his lips. Race back inside her own.

Luxuriate in textures and taste.

Time was not a factor. It seemed to stop with them inside a glass box of desire. His tongue dueled with hers and then retreated again. Hers chased and enticed.

Incredibly, Pam knew she was about to climax just on the basis of this one kiss that was like nothing she'd ever known.

Suddenly, touching his lips alone wasn't enough. Her hand began clenching and kneading his thigh and moving in a slow trek upwards. His moan of appreciation spurred her on. His hands moved from her arms to one breast where he stroked slowly in large circles that decreased with every turn around her, until it seemed as if every nerve ending in her body that wasn't in her mouth was rushing to that one breast.

Pam thought it could be her imagination, but it seemed every single feeling she had was wound tighter than ever before.

The coffee flavor lingering on his tongue was stronger, as if she were drinking the hot seductive brew from his mouth.

The way the tip of his tongue danced with hers felt as if it were so close it were her own. She swore there was a sizzle when their tongues met and mated.

The sizzle raced through her body and strummed against her labia lips as if his fingers were spreading her, preparing her for his mouth and tongue tracing her desire there.

Pam was no stranger to desire. She was a woman, a mother. She had a fleeting moment to wonder, though, before this kiss with this stranger spun even further out of control, if she'd ever before known a desire like this.

Part of her mind was reacting strongly. It was telling her she had to stop before this went any further. There was a voice inside her denying that thought. The voice of surrender was growing stronger and stronger with each passing second.

Without further thought, her hand moved higher. She ran her fingertips over the straining bulge behind his jeans. Seconds later, despite the fact her hand was still long inches away, the button at the waistband and the zipper were released. He wasn't wearing any underwear. *Oh, my,* she thought catching her breath on a gasp. His cock stood out from a bed of springy hair, proud, full, and glistening wetly at the tip. Her fingers swirled his seed around, coating her hand and spreading it evenly around the tip.

Her nails were short, no-nonsense to go with her callus-hardened hand. Suddenly, she wished she had the hands and nails of a pampered woman. She would dig those nails gently into his flesh, seeing what kind of reaction she could produce.

As if he could read her mind, Luke groaned again and, if possible, his cock swelled further. His hand squeezed her breast roughly. She didn't feel any pain. If anything, it only increased her desire.

"Luke," she gasped.

"I know," he agreed. "I have to have you. Now."

They dropped their hands from the other only long enough to undress. She had her jeans down to her knees when she heard his groan.

He tackled her and pinned her to the floor with his weight.

"I'm sorry." He groaned again. "Make me stop."

She shook her head as he stripped away the rest of her clothing. There were many things she could do, but making him stop wasn't one of them. Seconds later, he reached down, adjusted himself a bit and slid inside her pussy.

She caught her breath. She knew he was big, had seen his nine inches when he'd opened his jeans, but he was also wide. Just his tip was inside her and already she felt stretched. She began to panic. She was aroused, but now she was afraid she was not nearly aroused enough to take him to the hilt. And she wanted him as deep within her as possible.

As if sensing her trepidation, he began kissing her again. She could tell by the shivers rippling over his skin that it was taking every ounce of his control to give her time. Suddenly, it didn't matter. She knew she could take him. She knew she couldn't wait any longer. The thought flashed in her mind that it had been a hundred years of waiting, of dreaming, for this moment. She wouldn't be denied any longer.

She frowned a bit at the thought, but it was if someone else was controlling her body, if not her mind. Her thighs spread a bit allowing him to sink deeper between them. A little roll of her hips and his rock-hard penis inched forward.

He didn't need any other hints. His hips began thrusting. Soon her ears were roaring with the beats of her heart racing in tempo to the increasing fervor of his plunges into her body. He was overwhelming her with his size, his strength, the way it felt like his cock was touching every inch of her vagina. Her inner walls were grabbing at him, and every time he tried to withdraw even the slightest amount, they clung as if they would never let him go. Their bodies were so close his groin was grinding against her clit. It felt wonderful and terrifying at the same time.

She felt her eyes starting to cross as the pleasure began to roll through and over her like a tidal wave. The edge of darkness was hovering just above her and she strained to reach it. When his fingers reached up and pinched her turgid nipples, it sent her free-falling over the edge.

She heard his shout of satisfaction and felt the endless waves of his release as it crashed against the mouth of her womb.

As she lay in that suspended freefall she had the oddest feeling she could smell lavender wafting around them.

CHAPTER 2

Luke lay against his naked building inspector and wondered if he had truly gone mad.

He'd taken a stranger on the floor of his gutted bathroom. He'd taken a beautiful woman without care, without thought of anything but branding her as his. Now and forever more.

This was worse than his nighttime excursions because at least those only tortured his own soul. Now he'd brought someone else into his own hell. Worse, it was probably going to get him arrested.

Who could blame her?

She had come to do business. Instead she'd found herself taken by a madman.

As further proof of his loss of connection to reality, at the end, he swore he'd smelled lavender. He wondered if it came from her. His head lay against her breast and he sniffed. No lavender. Just soap. He shook his head. He had to get out of the trance and try to fix this somehow. But how did a man apologize for taking a woman without her choice? There was a word for that. He couldn't bring himself to admit it applied, but it still fit.

He didn't know how to start except by opening his mouth. "I'm…"

"If you apologize, I'm going to get really ticked off."

There was that voice again. Husky, warm, sexy. It was his undoing. He felt his cock responding and ruthlessly tamped it down. There would be no more of that.

"I should," he said instead.

"No, you shouldn't. Although, I don't know what came over me. I'm not the type to do this kind of thing. I didn't even do it in my wild teenage years. I certainly don't do it now." She paused, then smiled. It was a slow smile and lit her eyes making them seem incredibly large and attractive to him. "I do know what came in me, and it had everything to do with that incredible cock of yours."

Luke smiled slightly and pulled away with regret. Her body clung nicely to his and he knew it wouldn't take much more enticement to go another round. Despite her words and easy tone, he meant to have some control the next time around. There would be a next time. If he didn't go to jail, that is.

But for now, the parts of him wishing only to mate like a wolf would just have to be ignored. "How about if I apologize for the technique then?"

Pam hummed, then stretched her arms over her head. Luke watched the way her movements pulled her breasts up towards her chin. They were not his normal cup of tea. In fact, when all his friends were ogling the latest D-cup pinup he'd been looking at the legs. But he guessed with age came a certain degree of maturity. Or perhaps it was just because the ghost who'd been visiting him every night had been full-figured, but now Luke couldn't imagine wanting another woman with breasts any smaller.

"How'd I know she had big breasts?" he murmured.

"Excuse me?" The woman was looking at him now like he was headed to the loony bin. Perhaps she was right.

"Really, you probably won't believe this, but I usually show more finesse, more care about my partner's needs than I did just now," he said. "So how about I make it up to you tonight."

He paused. She'd said something about kids. Oh God, could she be married?

"Tonight? Yeah, I could do that." She smiled and said. "And no, I'm not married. Now."

Luke shook his head. Either everything he was thinking was visible on his face or this woman could read his mind.

"You're probably thinking I'm into mind reading or something, right?" she asked.

He could hear the humor in her voice. It was just one more thing that attracted him to her.

"Don't worry. Just because this is a haunted house, I'm no witch."

He pulled her into his arms and hugged her. "I don't know about that. You seem to have cast a spell over me."

"Hah. I think the one casting spells is you," she teased right back. "So how about we get dressed and finish our business? Then you can get ready for tonight."

He smiled at the gleam in her eyes. "Am I going to need a lot of preparation?"

She swept her eyes over him, her mouth turning up slightly at the sight of his long, lean body. His cock rose proudly when her appreciative gaze lingered there.

"No preparation exactly," she said, licking her lips. "I just want you to be rested up."

Luke laughed. She didn't know the half of it.

*   *   *

Later that morning, Luke found himself whistling as he worked with the drywall. It wasn't a job he normally relished. It was hard, messy and dusty. It didn't matter. All he could think about was the incredible morning he'd spent with Pam. He knew his men were looking at him oddly, wondering at the change in his temperament. He didn't care.

At one point, when he was alone in the bathroom, he felt the presence of his ghost behind him.

"Look, I appreciate the service, but I don't think I need you anymore," he murmured, turning slowly. It was probably his imagination, but he could almost make out her shape. Again, he had the feeling that she looked a lot like Pam. Was it wistful thinking? She hovered on one side of the door. It should have felt weird talking aloud to her but it didn't. So he continued.

"I'm sorry if you don't like what I'm doing here, but it can't be helped. I promise I'm going to take good care of the house. And you're welcome to continue living here as long as I own this house, but then you're just going to have to find someplace else to haunt. The new owners may not get it. But please, you have to stop coming around like this, just popping in. My friend from this morning probably wouldn't be comfortable with you, you know? I'm just going to have to ask you to trust me on this."

"Yo, boss?"

Luke started at the sound of his foreman's voice. He looked back at the door. The ghost was gone. Seconds later, his foreman stood in her place.

"What's going on? Talking to yourself?"

Luke laughed. "A little. It's these old houses, you know? Sometimes it feels like they're alive."

The foreman didn't look impressed. "You know, maybe you need to get out a little bit. Me and some of the guys are going out for a drink. Wanta come?"

Luke shook his head. "No. Actually I have a date."

"No shit? Where did you find time for picking up some girl? I didn't think you'd been anywhere but the home supply store since you'd been here."

"Well, actually the inspector and I kind of hit it off this morning. Her name's Pam Lukasiac. You know her?"

"Oh sure. Pam and her daddy are from here, you know? Well, that's great. She's a great gal. Kind of had it tough lately, but she knows her stuff."

"I thought so. When you say she's kind of had it tough, what do you mean?"

His foreman shrugged. "You know. The usual. Her father ran one of the best contracting firms around here. I used to work for him. He started having health problems and, instead of giving it to Pam like he should've, he turned it over to that lazy heel she was married to."

"He didn't know what he was doing?" Luke asked.

"Well, now, that's a matter of opinion. I think he knew exactly what he was doing. He's a crook, that one, always looking for the angle that's going to get him the biggest pot."

"You have a problem making money?" Luke asked lightly. Since the foreman and his crew were charging Luke a small fortune to help him with the drywall, he couldn't imagine that.

"Heck, no. We all gotta make a living. But I don't cotton to cutting corners so much that you make things dangerous. That's what Pam's ex did."

Luke felt a little burn of tension in his stomach. He could see his ghost starting to form again, this time right next to his foreman. But the man seemed totally oblivious.

"Maybe Pam and her father were in agreement with what her husband did. It wouldn't be the first time a contractor got greedy."

The foreman frowned. "Well, you must not have figured too much out about Pam earlier if you think that. She's as honest as a day is long."

"Yeah, but what about her father?" Luke asked.

"Nah. He's a cursed son of a gun, but he's so straight and honest you could stick a poker up his butt. No, what Lukasiac did was all on his own."

"So, what happened?"

"Well, the guy just messed things up enough to get Pam and her father sued. Then he vanished. Long gone. They had to sell everything out just to settle the case. Now, Pam's struggling, working two or three jobs just to keep them afloat."

Luke nodded. "Is her father very sick?"

"Yeah. That's the rub. He's got Alzheimer's. He doesn't know what's going on. So, it's just Pam and her little boy." The man paused. "Look, I don't know you very well. You seem like an upright kind of guy to work for."

"Thank you," Luke said.

"But don't you go messing with Pam if you aren't serious, you hear? That girl doesn't need any more trouble."

Luke straightened and looked at the man. He narrowed his eyes. "You seem to care a lot for her. Are you looking to step in for her husband?"

The foreman laughed. "Nah. I got me a wife and she's all I can handle. I think of Pam as my little sister. So do all the other guys in my crew. I'm just trying to give you a little friendly advice."

Luke nodded. Well, it was a good thing these guys hadn't arrived about an hour earlier when he and Pam were going at it like minks on the floor. He had a feeling they wouldn't have been so easy to get along with.

He shook his head. He couldn't think about what might have been. He had to worry about going forward. Pam hadn't been angry about his actions and had taken responsibility for her part. Besides, he wasn't looking for a relationship. He was just looking to make a bit of amends with a woman who'd been a good sport.

He ignored the little voice inside him that called him a liar.

*   *   *

I can't believe I'm going to do this, Pam thought as she got ready for her date with Luke St. Clair. She'd dropped her son, Johnny, off at the sitter's and now was pacing in her living room. She wondered again at her choice of clothes. She was wearing a long flowered skirt and a simple T-shirt. Her legs were bare, partially in favor of the late August heat wave shrouding the area, but mostly because, truth be told, Pam didn't own a pair of nylons. It wasn't like she'd had any use for them lately.

She had fallen into the harried Mom wardrobe—jeans and tees—the last six months. It had been comfortable, durable and easy. Now she was thinking she should have paid more attention to herself.

She looked critically in the mirror off the entry hall. Would he think her dumpy? She started to head back to her closet, even knowing it was a useless trip, when the sound of a car pulling in her driveway stopped her. He was here. She wiped suddenly damp hands on the material of her skirt and thrust her chin up. There was no reason for nerves. She'd already been more intimate with him than she'd been with anyone else since Sonny had left. Besides, this was just dinner and whatever. It wasn't marriage.

Pam blew out a breath, pasted a smile on her lips and opened the door.

He'd brought her flowers. Not roses but a clutch of lavender. She thought of the lavender she'd smelled while in his bathroom. She hadn't seen any near his house, but that didn't mean it wasn't planted there. The fact he'd gone to the trouble brought a smile to her face.

"Hi," she said.

"Hi yourself," he answered. "You look great!"

"Thanks," she said. She bit her lip against the urge to downplay the outfit. She wasn't going to allow any insecurity to show through now. "And thanks for those. How'd you know lavender was my favorite?"

For a second Luke looked like he didn't know what she was talking about. Then he snapped back with a smile. "Oh, I don't know. It was just something that came to me."

She smiled in return. "Well, thanks. Come on in and I'll get something to put those in."

She turned and went back to her kitchen. He followed behind her.

"This is a great place. Is it your family home?"

"Yes. My father built it thirty years ago," Pam said.

"Are your parents still alive?" he asked.

"Just my father. He's in a nursing home. He's got Alzheimer's."

"That's tough," Luke said. He leaned against the countertop while she found a vase, poured in water and the flowers in it. "So, do you have any children?"

"Yes. Johnny. He's five."

Luke smiled. "Five. That's a great age. Is his father around?"

Pam frowned. "No. It's just Johnny, me, and of course, Pops. That's the way we like it."

There was a few seconds of humming silence. Pam was grateful when Luke didn't press.

In fact, for the next two hours, he was the perfect, charming date. He took her to a nice, family-owned Italian restaurant in the nearby town of Hamburg. They shared a bottle of red, excellent seafood Alfredo, and lively, interesting conversation.

She learned they had a lot more in common than just an obvious appreciation of fine architecture. They both loved Bogie and Bacall movies—his favorite was *The Big Sleep*, and hers was *To Have and Have Not*. They shared a passion for electronic gadgets and the original *Star Trek* television series.

It was over a shared cannoli that he convinced her to tell him more about the ghost of Knob Hill.

"So, come on now, you've got to tell me more about this ghost in my house," he said.

His eyes were that warm hazel again as he leaned back against the chair back. She watched the way his fingers played with the stem of his wineglass. They were strong, but she remembered vividly, they were not abusive. The thought of the way he'd stroked and pinched her breasts with just the right amount of pressure made her wriggle a bit in her own chair.

"Ah, I just know the legend. Honestly, you'd get the complete story from the historical society."

He waited.

She sighed. "Oh, all right. Although, if you truly think you've seen the ghosts, you should just probably ask them yourself."

When he still didn't respond, she sighed again. "Oh, okay. The story is that your house was built as a brothel to service the sailors on the ships that traveled the lakes. It was even supported by the Buffalo city government at the time because they thought if the brothel was out here, away from the city, the sailors wouldn't be quite so rambunctious once they got into town. They were gearing up for the 1901 Exposition at the time, so the politicians were very interested in making Buffalo safe for all the visitors they expected."

Luke smiled. "It's funny, isn't it? It doesn't matter the era, politicians are always looking for ways to make their lot better."

Pam laughed. "You better believe it. Don't get me going on the way the system works now. It's a joke. Anyway, back to the ghost story...

"As the story goes, everything was fine. The brothel was a huge success. But one of the ladies fell in love with one of her visitors. They say he fell for her as well. He was a captain of one of the ships and promised on his next trip to Buffalo, he'd marry her and take her to live on the high seas with him."

Luke nodded. "Let me guess. He never returned?"

"That's right. Now, this lady was very popular with the visitors. The story says she was small and blonde with eyes the color of Lake Erie's glass-smooth waters."

"I can see why she'd be popular then," Luke murmured.

Pam felt the way his eyes roved over her own blonde hair, which she'd let hang down her back tonight, before lighting on her own eyes.

"There is something about a blonde, blue-eyed woman."

Pam felt the desire, which had been happily simmering inside her, kick it up a bit. His eyes had that languid sex appeal again. She wondered if she touched her bare foot to his leg, if they would turn hazel or something else.

Fanning herself with her cloth napkin instead of doing what she wanted, she said, "Wow, it's getting hot in here. I think they need to turn up the air."

He just gave her that smile again and she knew he wasn't falling for the hot flash bit.

"Anyway, it's said our heroine was determined to be true to her lover. So she refused to take any more clients. She locked herself in her room, which was the front bedroom where you're putting your master suite, and refused to come out. She spent every day looking out her windows, waiting and watching for her man to return from the sea."

"What happened then?" Luke asked.

Pam shrugged. "According to legend, they called the sheriff and he went in after her. There was a scuffle, and she apparently fell to her death from the window. They say, as she fell, she vowed she would walk the halls of the house for all her days until her lover returned."

Luke scratched the side of his nose. "Well, that explains the bit about walking the halls. Did her beloved sailor ever return?"

"Yes. He came back just a few weeks after her death. Not only did it turn out he was a ship's captain, but he was also the son of the family who owned the shipping line. He had been captaining their ships to get experience and had gone back to his family to tell them he had met his bride. It seemed it took some convincing, but finally they agreed with his decision.

"He was not happy when he returned to learn what had happened to his fiancée. The story goes he was livid and took great care to let all the city officials know it. Since his family was so rich, they forced the brothel to close and he put so much pressure on the area officials that the owner of the brothel lost everything.

"The captain is said to have promised that no one would ever be able to make a success of any building on this land until he could hold his beloved in his arms once again."

Luke was quiet for a few moments. "So...you're telling me my house is haunted and cursed?"

Pam laughed. "Well, that's one way to look at it."

Luke joined her. "Well, it's a good thing I wasn't planning on making this a hotel or resort then, huh?"

Pam smiled and then the conversation moved in a different direction as they talked about some of the latest advancements in electronic home security and safety devices.

Much later, as she leaned back against the passenger seat of his car, replete with good food, wine and conversation, she was only mildly surprised that, instead of taking a right turn to her house, he took the left to his.

When they drove to the top of the hill, Pam told herself it was her imagination she saw someone standing at one of the third floor windows watching as they drove up.

She quickly forgot it though when he put the car into park. He paused, then reached for her hand, turning the palm upwards to his mouth. He placed a soft kiss in the middle as his beautiful eyes locked onto hers.

Not for the first time since meeting Luke, Pam wished she were something she wasn't. She devoutly wished in that moment her hands were those of a pampered woman, hands that would be able to caress his lips, face, and much, much lower with tender softness.

That wasn't her lot in life. She was a woman more used to holding a power saw than lavender bouquets. She felt the nerves kick up in her stomach. She needed to stop this before it went any further. She needed to stop this before he broke her heart.

Before she could put her thoughts into words, he spoke. "You are so beautiful to me," he murmured.

His lips moved against her palm, sending a riot of emotion rocking through her. He wetly traced the outline of the lines and blisters. When he bit lightly on the pad of her thumb where she'd scraped it that afternoon on his inspection, she felt something loosen deep in her core.

She knew no matter what, she wouldn't be ending this. Not before she had the chance to be with him one more time. After that…well, she'd deal with tomorrow when tomorrow came.

"I'd like you to come in with me," he said. "I'd like you to stay the night with me. I know that's probably not going to happen. I know you have responsibilities."

He paused and took a deep breath. It sounded to Pam like he was a swimmer getting ready to dive to the bottom of a lake.

"I know I don't deserve a second chance, but I'd like you to give me one. I want you to give me anything you can."

Pam took her free hand and placed her fingers against his lips, stopping his words.

"And I want the same thing," she said. "Please make love to me, Luke. Again."

He closed his eyes and then opened them quickly. He pulled her into his arms and kissed her on her mouth.

It felt just like coming home to Pam. A home she'd felt only one other time in her life, earlier that afternoon on the floor of his bathroom.

The windows were starting to fog when they finally separated. He got out of the car and hurried around the vehicle to open her door. She felt a little like Cinderella being returned from the ball. He took her hand to help her from the car then led her into the house. It was dark and a little eerie, but his warmth and strength was a good grounding for her. When she had told him the legend about the house, she hadn't told him everything. She hadn't told him just how personal it was to her. Nor had she told him that she fully believed the legend.

She remembered coming to Knob Hill several times in her life and always feeling a strong connection to it. The connection wasn't fear exactly, but more of a feeling that someone or something was watching her. As long as he held her hand in his, all she felt was a driving need that was bordering on painful.

He led her up the two flights of stairs and turned her to the massive front master bedroom. At the stage of construction where he was, it was almost completely empty. The lone furniture there sent a thrill through Pam, though.

Luke had already built a large pedestal bed frame. She could see a king-sized mattress with a deep chocolate-colored quilt and matching sheets. The sheets were tossed back as if he had jumped out of bed that morning in a hurry.

She licked her suddenly dry lips at the thought of rushing him back into that bed right now. Beside the bed was an upside down crate with small lamp on it.

The very lack of furnishings made the view from the huge, albeit unfinished, windows even more startling. The sun was hanging low in the sky over the lake and poured through the windows like spun gold. Pam moved closer to the windows and tried to calm her racing heart.

He stepped behind her and wrapped his arms around her waist. She felt his chin on her shoulder and she shifted her head to one side giving his lips access to her neck. Instead of kissing there, he traced her ear lobe with his hot tongue. When he took the lobe into his mouth and bit gently, Pam's hands reached up to move his, content to rest just below her breasts, up until he was cupping them.

Still suckling her lobe, he played finger games on each breast tracing light circles up and over them before finally stroking the outline of her nipples, which were already growing hard. Much too soon for Pam's thinking, his hands left her breasts and moved down her stomach below her navel until the tips of his fingers were resting just at her pubic line.

His breath whispered in her ear. "You're so beautiful," he said. "I've dreamed of you standing here like this."

Pam felt her breath clutch and stutter in her lungs.

"May I give you pleasure?" he asked.

Pam felt part of her melting. No other man had ever simply asked that before. She felt as if he was now reaching more than just her body—he was touching her soul as well. She wanted to say yes. But her voice was suddenly lost to her. All she could do was moan. Thankfully he interpreted the sound correctly.

His fingers moved again and, before she could catch her breath, he had removed her skirt and tee-shirt. Her bra came next and she was about to help him remove her panties when he stopped her.

"No. Let me just touch you," he murmured.

He was on his knees now, still behind her. She felt a little odd standing in front of those windows dressed only in her panties and sandals, but those feelings quickly vanished when he began to touch her again. His hands returned to her abdomen. They were forming a vee against the silk of her panties, his fingers resting just above her mound. His hands began a slow, erotic massage against her and made her feel incredibly warm.

It was so arousing she began to think she could feel those warm hands all the way to her ovaries. She took a deep breath on the sensation and it was like she'd taken a quick gulp of some potent wine the way the heat flared through her bloodstream and rushed to her brain on a little sexual high.

Then she felt his lips caressing down her spine until they were resting against the indentation of her butt. Seconds later she felt the stroke of his tongue there and jerked in reaction.

"Would you like me to stop?" he asked.

"Uhmm, no. I just wasn't expecting it," she replied.

His soft chuckle blew against her and she almost shivered in response.

"Good. Unexpected is good."

His hands moved again, this time sliding under the elastic waistband of her panties and finally touching her skin. His fingers toyed with the top edge of her pubis. She caught her breath again. She was so excited she was almost ready to explode and he hadn't even reached her clit yet.

She felt the bite of his teeth, gentle on the base of her spine, instantly followed by the brush of his tongue easing away the tiny bit of pain. Then his fingers slipped inside her vagina and went unerringly to the small bump on the front wall.

"Ahh," she gasped as his fingers pushed and pressed against the spot with uncanny accuracy. She felt as if she was ready to orgasm and felt her clit swell even more. Her vision started to gray, which had to be why she thought she saw a figure forming in the room. It was white tendrils laced with wisps of gray hovering just to the left of them. Then his fingers moved again and she couldn't concentrate on anything but what he was doing to her body.

"Please, Luke," she gasped.

He swept her panties down off her hips and let them fall to her ankles.

"Bend over," he instructed.

Mindless, wanting everything, anything he offered, she did.

His hands reached to her and spread her pussy lips apart. She felt his breath, then his tongue as it traced its way down her butt, flicked tentatively at her crack before spearing inside her pussy. His fingers did a dance across the spot he'd found moments before, rubbing and squeezing the hard button of her desire while his tongue danced around her clit. Her orgasm began like a flood and was soon washing her away. She threw her head back and howled.

Her legs were so shaky she would have fallen into a puddle of mindless satiation except he held her upright, soothing her from the high slowly back to normal with light strokes across her mound and whispered words against her spine.

Finally she was able to move. She turned in his arms and saw him smile up at her. His mouth was gleaming with the evidence of her release. When she looked down, she saw how his cock was straining against his pants.

She got down on her knees and began removing his clothes. First she unbuttoned his shirt. His chest was something to dream over. Tanned and strong without being muscle-bound, it was a sensory delight for her fingers. She pushed his shirt aside as her hands moved across his shoulder and down his pecs, which were flexing in delight. She fingered his small, hard nipple and then rested her lips against it. She bit lightly and he groaned in reply. Then she did the same thing to the left side.

He had a line of hair racing straight down his chest and she followed that line with her teeth and tongue until she reached the waistband of his pants. While she unbuttoned the fly, she used her tongue to rim his navel, plunging in and out in a pantomime of the sex act she hoped they would share later.

Finally his pants were open and she could see the outline of him underneath the satin fabric of his boxers. She stroked her hand over him, measuring him and taking delight in how he grew with just a single touch.

"Let me get you undressed," she murmured, moving back to allow Luke to stand up. He stepped out of his pants and underwear and she stayed on her knees looking up at him. His cock was tilted straight north towards his chest, but Pam wanted to give him a little more foreplay before she brought him his first release.

She took his balls in her hands and gently caressed them, keeping her touch light but hypnotic. She traced a finger down the cord of tissue between his sack and lower until she could almost reach his butt, and then brought her finger back to the starting point. Then she used her tongue to trace the same pathway.

By the time her mouth reached the top of his sac again, he was groaning and thrusting his hips toward her.

She crawled over to the bed and lay down on her back with her head hanging slightly over the edge. She waited for the blood to stop rushing to her brain, then said to him, "Come here, Luke."

He walked over to her and stood. She took his cock in her hand and pulled it to her. She started slow, running her tongue over the slit, reveling in the taste of his come before she opened her mouth wider. He began thrusting and she took as much of him as she could.

"Oh, God," he groaned as he eagerly fucked her mouth.

She felt his tension grow and reached up with her hands to hold his cock straight as he pounded deeper and deeper inside her mouth. She felt his balls swell then tasted the sweet ecstasy of his seed as he exploded against her tongue.

His orgasm seemed to go on forever. Some of his cum overflowed her lips before he finally pulled away.

"Uhmm," she said, licking the residue from her lips. "Just the way I like my dessert."

He fell to his knees and took her mouth with his own, catching her words and sharing the lingering taste of his release with her. As his tongue dueled with hers, Pam felt something move over her.

She flet a sense of power and longing that had nothing to do with the present and everything to do with the past. Since she'd first met him here in this house, she'd felt differently than she ever had. It was almost as if she was being controlled by something or someone else. For years, she'd been wondering if she'd ever find the illusive spark that made life special. She'd also wondered if she would ever be able to fulfill the prophecy of her ancestors. Now she knew everything was the way it had been meant for a hundred years.

She should have been frightened, angry at the very least. All she felt was relief. She felt that finally she was righting some wrong. She didn't know why, but she knew loving this man at this time was her destiny, which had long been denied.

Suddenly, she laughed.

Luke pulled away and looked at her. "What was that about?"

She just shook her head. "You probably won't understand."

He pushed her back against his mattress and then lay beside her. He ran his hand across her breasts and she sucked in her breath. It was incredible what he could do to her with a single touch.

"No secrets," he said. "Tell me what made you laugh."

"Okay. I was just thinking about all this." She waved her hand, encompassing the house, the room and them. "Have you thought about it?"

He looked down at her. "You mean the fact we seem like we're combustible when we come together?"

Pam chewed on her bottom lip. She wasn't sure if she wanted to continue this discussion. How could she not?

"Has it ever been like that for you before?"

His fingers stilled. "I don't know exactly what you mean."

"I mean have you ever felt this urgency before?"

He opened his mouth to answer then closed it again. "No. Well, at least not with this frequency since I was about twelve."

Pam caught her breath. "This will sound strange, but have your dreams been...well...different lately?"

He pulled a little away from her and looked down at her. "How do you mean?"

But Pam saw the answer in his eyes. "You've had visitors, haven't you? That's what you meant this morning when you said you'd seen the ghosts." The last wasn't a question.

"Yes. Since the first night I stayed here." He paused. "No, that isn't true. Fact is, I 'saw' this house in a dream before I even knew it existed."

"Saw it?"

"Yes. I dreamed this house was standing on this knoll overlooking Lake Erie. When I woke up, I searched the Internet for Lake Erie properties and found it. I offered the asking price and the sale was completed in less than a week."

Pam nodded. "What's happened since you've been here?"

Luke shifted as if embarrassed. "I've been having some pretty erotic fantasies."

"Fantasies? Or something else?"

Luke frowned. "I honestly don't know. At first, I thought they were just dreams. But they're so real. It's like she's in the room with me."

Pam smiled. "Is there anything familiar about her to you?"

"Yes. When you showed up this morning, at first I thought you were her."

Pam laughed and hugged him to her. "Ahh. That explains the look on your face and..."

"And the fact that I had a raging hard-on?"

"Uh-huh. Don't worry. I didn't hold it against you."

Luke groaned at her pun. "See, that's where you women have it all wrong. I would've gladly held it against you. I'd like to hold it against you again now."

He playfully rolled over on top of her. Her legs parted and he settled into the vee of her pelvis, his cock sliding just inside her pussy lips as if it had been tailored to fit there. They simultaneously sighed at the sensation.

After a moment of savoring their position, he added, "You sound like you've been experiencing something as well."

Pam smiled and ran her hand over his face. "Yes. I've been dreaming of you."

"Of me or my ghost?" He ran a hand down her breast and settled on circling her nipple with his finger. He smiled almost absently when it puckered in response. She flexed her hips slightly, tightening her walls around his tip and causing his breath to hitch. She smiled as well, enjoying the feel of power rushing through her.

When his lips met hers, she lost all ability to think. She knew only that there was no him, no her. No past. No future. Just them, mated together in perfect harmony in a moment suspended in ecstasy. She was his, and he was hers for all time.

*   *   *

The moon was setting when they finally got around to finishing their conversation. They were feeding each other the breakfast of gods, fresh grapes and dried dates. In between bites, Luke said, "You never answered my question before."

Pam smiled and stretched luxuriously. She should have been exhausted since they hadn't slept a moment, but she felt simply revived.

"You want to know if I was dreaming of you or a ghost?" she asked.

"Yes."

"It was you. When you opened the door this morning, I knew exactly what you were feeling because I was feeling the same thing. Thank God you didn't check my panties because you'd have known it as well."

He grinned. "I knew you were hot for me."

Pam laughed. They shared a kiss that was familiar but intense. "But I also saw a ghost."

"A man or woman?"

Pam bit her lip. "Both." She placed her fingers over his lips to stop the questions she could see in his eyes. "I've had a dream visitor coming to see me every night since I was a little girl. He is my great, great grandfather, and he has, over the years, told me the complete history of this house. His name was John, and he was a kind, gentle man who loved the woman of his dreams beyond death. I named my son after him."

Luke didn't say anything for a moment. "So you're the descendent of her lost love?"

"Yes. And my father, my family, owned this house. Great-great-Grandfather bought it twenty years after her death. He never lived here though. Claimed he couldn't. He also wouldn't let anyone change it in any way. We've kept it in the family until you bought it."

Luke blinked. "What do you think made the time right? I mean, how were you able to sell it now?"

"My great-great-grandfather has been visiting my dreams for the last six months telling me that a man would come from the west. He'd have new plans for the house and that I should sell it, no matter what he offered."

"But I'm stumped. How did you know it was me?" Luke asked. "There could be another man from the west."

"I dreamed of you as well. I dreamed of you making love to me. And every night for the last two weeks, instead of my great, great grandfather, I dreamed of you. You were so real, it was if you were touching me, making love to me."

Luke was silent for so long Pam began to think she'd made a huge mistake telling him all this. It would have probably been better to just let him think their ghosts were just normal, ordinary, unconnected ones.

Finally, a smile started slowly across Luke's face.

"Well, I guess there's only one answer. We'd better not let them down again. So I guess we're just going to have to stay in this house and make love until our dying days. That's the only way we're going put this ghost story to rest."

*   *   *

On a grassy knoll overlooking a Lake Erie shoal waits a fair maid.

Every day she looks out her high window to the west, to the south, to the north, hoping to see her true love's ship coming to take her away.

Weeks, months and years pass with the same sight.

And then one morning, his ship sails in just as the night is breaking into day. She runs to the dock to meet him and they make love for all eternity.

FRAMED IN DREAMS

CHAPTER 1

FOR SALE
Victorian era mansion overlooking Lake Ontario needs owner with
spirit and extra TLC to spare. View worth $10 million. Motivated seller
willing to relinquish for only $500k.

*   *   *

"Oh, my God, it's perfect." Helen Myers read the ad a second, then a third time. She could see herself sitting in a third floor luxury suite, looking out a bank of windows at the unending blue horizon from the vast lake and sky. Perhaps, on a clear day, she could see all the way to Canada.

After her daily meditation, she'd go downstairs and see to her guests. It would be the perfect blend of stylish sophistication and homey comfort.

She picked up her cell, and dialed the number without a second thought.

*   *   *

"Damn it. What idiot would pay their asking price?" Bert Vogl said as he slammed down the phone. "Don't they know the repairs alone are going to cost a fortune just to make it livable?"

"Hey, boss, what's up?" Kerry Jones was his niece and she was sweet, impossibly cheerful and his all around girl Friday at Vogl Construction. She'd only been working for him for three months after her graduation, but he didn't know how he'd ever survived running the business without her. But the last thing he wanted now was her cheerful outlook.

Vogl Construction, which had started out just him and his hands, was now a growing concern. He had two crews working full-time in the summer and one that worked year around. Lately, though, he'd begun to miss the old days when it was just him and his tools. Maybe that's why this latest development stung so badly.

"Somebody bought the old Borrelli place," he said.

Kerry's eyes got huge. "You're kidding? While you were in Mexico?"

"Yes. Apparently they gave the estate the asking price. What kind of idiot would do that?"

Kerry frowned. "That doesn't make any sense."

"No, it makes absolute sense. It's probably some commercial group going to raze the place and put up condos that look just like every other unit in the world. They'll put twenty or thirty on the lot, sell 'em for a mil each and be done."

Kerry chewed on her lip. "I don't think it was a commercial concern, boss."

"That's what it has to be," Bert raged. "Nobody else would pay that kind of money if they just wanted to live in it. Heck, even rich fools have lawyers to keep them from sinking cash into a money pit like that."

"I don't know, boss," Kerry said. "I got this message just a little while ago. It didn't make sense, but now it does."

"What message?"

"It's from a Helen Myers. She's looking for a contractor to handle some work. She gave the address. It didn't register before, but it's the Borrelli house. I bet she's the one who bought it."

Bert rolled his eyes. "Oh, Jeezus. Let me guess. She wasn't from around here, was she?"

"No. Her number on the caller id was a Manhattan area code."

Bert shook his head. "Just wonderful. Ab-so-freak-in' wonderful."

*   *   *

Helen sat in the front seat of her car and looked at her house. She wanted to cry, but knew crying wouldn't do a bit of good. Her dream house was a nightmare.

From where she was sitting, she could see gaping holes in the roof.

A narrow balcony that may have once been quaint was hanging lop-sided from the third floor to midway down the second floor windows and looked as if the next stiff wind would blow it right off. The shingles, which were curved in the Victorian style, were rotting. As she watched, what looked like a million large black insects gathered around several on the third level.

The front porch, which probably at one time went the length of the front, was only halfway across it now. It hadn't been torn down, but had fallen off. She could see the debris lying like a pyre off to one side.

Helen put her head on the steering wheel for a few moments. Then she opened the door and got out of the car, walking toward the house. Well, maybe the inside wasn't as bad. She raised her head and wiped away the wetness. That's it. The inside couldn't be as bad. Soon the contractor she'd called to come give her an estimate would be here. He'd probably tell her the house just needed some cosmetic fixes.

Helen turned. One thing was certain. The view was everything it had been cracked up to be. As she stood at the top of the steep hill, where the graveled drive formed a parking circle, she looked out over the deep, glistening blue of Lake Ontario. For a moment, just a moment, Helen thought this view had been exactly the same for hundreds of years. For now, it was hers. The thought brought her an immediate sense of calm and peace, along with a return of optimism.

Feeling stronger, more in control of her future than she had for years, Helen turned back and faced her house, feeling a little like Mary Tyler Moore in the opening credits of her television show. She could make this work. It might be hard, but that would only make it more special when she achieved her dream.

Feeling like a girl again, she twirled, spreading her arms out wide and letting the vision of her house and lake merge with the way she dreamed they one day would.

*   *   *

Bert looked at the woman walking toward him. Whew, she was gorgeous. She very well could be the most beautiful woman he'd ever seen, and that was saying something.

Long, ash blonde hair trailed down her back, blue eyes rivaled the blue of the calm lake, and she had a figure that, well, she could be on a pin-up poster and make every man alive want to get up close and personal. Real personal. In fact, just watching as she walked toward him, he could feel his engines starting to purr and his libido sending out urgent messages that his Johnson was picking up readily. She had tiny little laugh lines at the corners of her eyes and mouth telling him she'd lived a little and the roundness of her figure also told him she'd enjoyed life. Man, oh, man, this was a woman who made him want to just hunker down and lose himself in her depths. He could see her in his mind, head thrown back, hips thrust forward taking every inch of his rock hard penis and giving him a welcome that would warm him from the inside out and drain his dick dry.

He reminded himself why he was here. Of course, there was nothing that said he couldn't try to screw her first.

His body agreed wholeheartedly with that idea.

"Mr. Vogl, I hope," she said. "I'm Helen Myers. As you can see, I have a few problems."

Warm brandy mixed with delicious cream was how her voice sounded. His body was telling him that laying right down on the ground and taking her had a lot of merit.

"I'm Vogl," he said, over a suddenly dry throat. "What are you looking for exactly? A house inspection?"

She chewed on her bottom lip as if she didn't know how to answer that. Bert was immediately hard as he watched small, white teeth emerge and nip at the naturally red skin of her lips. He had an overwhelming urge to place his tongue on those lips and just dive in— not for long, maybe a month or two—and see if they tasted like the juicy, ripe cherries they resembled.

"I don't think I need an inspection, but I would like an estimate on how to fix the place a bit."

A bit? Who was she kidding? But he wasn't going to tip his hand yet. First, he could use a little eye candy. Even if he had an idea she'd be too rich for his blood. But, hey, a quick bite or two wouldn't kill a guy.

Second, a quick glance at her ring finger showed no rings or marks. That didn't mean she wasn't married, but he was old-fashioned enough to think if she was and had just spent five hundred grand on a monstrosity, her mate would be here looking it over. By the looks of her late-model sedan, she had a lot of her belongings in the back seat and trunk. Still he wasn't a poacher. Never had been and wasn't about to start now.

"Okay," he said, "I can take a look. Are you the sole owner or do you have a partner? If your partner needs a report as well, I can send you two copies of the written version."

"No, it's just me," she replied. "I'm new to the area. I just closed on the place last week. I'm from Manhattan originally."

Bingo. Come to papa. Maybe he could tell her he'd deliver the report at dinner tonight. There was a scenic restaurant over in nearby Lewiston right on the river. He could see it all. Wine, scampi and sex. Then he'd tell her just how much it would cost to fix this place up.

She continued speaking and he paid attention rather than tasting the words as they came off her lips, which was what part of him wanted to do.

"You're not going to wait and just give me a written estimate, are you?"

"Er, no. I can give you a general idea," he answered. "But I'll need to go back and figure out the labor and materials exactly at the office. Is this your first time?"

For a moment she looked non-plused.

"Owning a home," he clarified.

"Oh, yes. This is my first time."

He smiled again, hoping she wouldn't think he was showing his teeth like a hungry wolf spotting an unprotected lamb.

"Okay, let's get started."

Bert knew it was perverse of him, but he drew the inspection out as long as possible. He went over every inch of the house as if he'd never been inside it before. But he gave her credit. For a naïve New Yorker, she was a quick study. When he pulled open the fuse box and she saw the way the old screw-in fuses were piggybacked, along with the open wires inside, she gasped.

"That doesn't look good," she said.

"Nah, but don't worry. This house was built in 1880, so it isn't supposed to look good by today's standards."

She chewed on her bottom lip again. "Is it a fire hazard? I mean, I turned on the lights upstairs."

Again, he had that urge to soothe the small tooth prints. "Well, it's probably okay, as long as you don't try to hook up anything like a microwave or toaster oven," he said. "But we don't want to let it go on too long, that's for sure. When they built this place, they didn't have any idea how many things were going to require electricity."

When her teeth went to work on her lip again, he almost groaned. He was feeling…he didn't know, kinda protective, along with aroused as well. How the hell did that happen? He didn't normally feel protective to any woman who wasn't related by blood.

She's the enemy, he reminded himself. At least as far as the house was concerned.

He tossed that thought aside and continued the inspection.

*   *   *

Oh, God, Helen thought as she followed Bert around her house. She was getting a sinking feeling in the pit of her stomach. She was trying to stay positive, but it was getting tougher and tougher as each minute ticked past.

All she could think of was the voice of her boss, Ramon Martinez, when she'd quit her job at the Manhattan Arms.

"You? Run a bed and breakfast? What a hoot," he'd said. "Oh, my darling, where in the world did you get such a silly idea? You can hardly run your own bank account. Why do you think you've never had the auditor job here?"

Helen remembered, frowning. She'd worked in the hotel business for fifteen years and had done just about every job in the business as she was working her way up the ladder. Before she'd given up two weeks ago, she had reached assistant manager. Ramon was the manager. He had never let her handle the auditor duties, however.

"I don't know. I just assumed it was something you were saving for me until this year," she had replied.

"Darling, please, I wouldn't let you touch my books with a ten-foot pole. You bounced a check, for Christ's sake."

"Excuse me? Once, five years ago. And then only because of a clerical error," she said scathingly. Ramon was a class A asshole. Too bad she hadn't figured that out until after she slept with him.

"There can be no mistakes when you run a business, darling. Face it—you're a knockout, you're a passable chef and you're excellent at customer relations. But as a financial manager, you're an airhead."

Helen had fumed. "What does that have to do with running my own place? It sounds to me like I have all but one of the necessary qualities. I can learn the other one. Or hire someone to handle it."

Ramon had laughed again. It sounded cruel to Helen. "Right. Well go. I can tell I'm not going to be able to talk you out of it. But I will make a prediction. You'll be back here begging me for a job in less than two months. Perhaps I'll give it to you. With a pay cut, of course."

Now Helen was wondering if perhaps Ramon had been right. She was standing back in front of her house when Vogl turned to her.

"Okay, Ms. Myers, you've got more than a few problems."

"I gathered as much," she said. Her contractor was something special. Where Ramon had all those dark, sensuous Latin looks, Vogl had to be of Irish descent with his shock of red hair and startling blue eyes. What's more, what he did to his worn jeans ought to be criminal. A couple times, when he'd bent down to check out the plumbing under the sink for instance, Helen had gotten a hot flash to beat the band at the way the material had molded his truly spectacular ass.

Used to men who wore suits like they were born in them, Vogl's muscular build, which she could tell had nothing to do with workouts at pricey clubs, was like a jolt of one hundred percent per caffeine to her libido. But she didn't call him here for sex, as appealing as that thought was at this moment.

As she looked at him now, she did what she always did when faced with something unpleasant. She cut to the chase.

"What's the bottom line?" she asked.

"Well, I'll have to go back to the office to get an exact estimate on supplies and figure the labor costs."

Helen nodded. "So you said earlier. But tell me what exactly we're looking at in terms of repairs and a ballpark figure."

"Well, the electrical is completely shot. I'd hoped maybe we'd just have to switch the box over to breakers, which would've only been about fifteen hundred."

Helen's spirits lifted. If she skipped a few meals, which she could certainly afford, and settled for using the rather dated, but hopefully functional, appliances the house came with rather than the commercial ones she'd hoped to buy, it might work.

"But the fuse box is the least of your concerns. The wiring throughout the entire house is shot. We'll have to take out walls and rewire everything."

"Oh, God," Helen said.

"Hey, like I said, this house is over a hundred and twenty years old. The wiring was probably done in the forties. Of course no one has lived here in five years, so it probably wasn't a priority to fix it. It's three stories, has five bedrooms, the dining room, kitchen, parlor. The one bathroom is a wreck, so you're going to need to add a couple of more. I'm guessing five grand for the electrical."

"Oh, God," Helen repeated.

"Now, you've also got the furnace. It's coming in on summer, so you probably can hold off on that, but I'd say you're going to have another five grand there, especially if you're going to want to add air."

"Oh, God," Helen repeated and sank down to the ground.

"Then—now this is just an estimate—but the plumbing is cast iron and stainless steel. That's what caused the green-black tint when we ran water in the sink. Plastic and cooper isn't too expensive, but it's going to cost a bit to take out the old stuff. That cast iron is a bear to break up. I'm going to go a little high on this because I don't want to underestimate how long it will take to remove those pipes. To replace them all, I'm thinking another eight to ten grand."

He paused and frowned as if he just realized her reaction.

"Hey, I'm sorry, Ms. Myers. I thought you knew what to expect."

"No." Helen willed her tears to stay back. "So you're saying twenty thousand dollars just to fix three things?"

"Well, yeah. Those are the immediate problems. You're also got the roof and the windows. About half of them have dry rot, so that'll probably add another twenty grand to the total. If you want to put all new vinyl siding on that's probably two or so more on top of that. The good news is they make some amazing stuff now that'll keep the look of the era, but are much easier to keep up.

"There's only one bathroom in this house and it's in pretty bad shape. Remodeling for an upscale bathroom runs about ten grand. If you're looking to add another full bath to the house that's probably fifty."

"Thousand?" Helen asked weakly.

"Yeah," he answered. "The rest of the inside is in pretty good shape, all things considered. The floors are in great shape for their age. But you still have a couple of choices there. You can put in all new laminate, which is easier to care for and runs about a dollar to a buck-fifty a square foot.

"Or you can buy a buffer and do it the old-fashioned way. These are all oak floors so they'll look pretty damn good when they're all polished. But you're going to have to sand them down first, then treat and buff them. It's not particularly expensive, but it is time-consuming and something you should consider doing fairly regularly to keep them up. That's your call.

"Then you've got some minor problems in the rooms. There's a disturbing amount of stucco on the ceilings. That's a messy fix and you probably want to strip off all the wall paper and go with just paint. Again, it's messy but not very costly. Probably less than five grand there."

Helen didn't know why, but the buck-fifty a square foot was the straw that broke her back. She covered her face with her hands and just started crying her heart out.

*   *   *

Damn, Bert thought. She's balling. What the hell do I do now?"

"Hey, hey, hey. Don't cry." He sat beside her and put his hand on her shoulder, attempting to offer her some comfort. She just cried harder. "Come on now. It's not all that bad. You just take one job at a time. Once you get the electrical and plumbing done, things will start looking better."

"You don't understand," she cried.

"Well, tell me," he said, feeling useless. He hated this. Every time his sister or mother cried he wanted to do whatever he could to stop it. "Tell me what's got you so upset."

"I spent almost all my money buying this place. I figured under five thousand dollars would be enough to get everything ready," she sobbed. "I've got fifty-five hundred to my name."

"You paid cash for this place?" he asked, incredulously.

She just nodded her head and cried harder.

Hell, he didn't know what to say. Now would be the perfect time to make his offer, but she was crying so hard he didn't think she would hear it. He wondered if she was getting hysterical. He continued to pat her shoulder, but she continued weeping. So he did the only thing he could think of to make her stop. He pulled her into his lap right there on the sagging porch, pulled her hands away from her face and kissed her until the crying stopped.

Her lips were soft and juicy. He tasted the salt of her tears and the ripeness of those cherries he'd wondered about earlier. When his tongue swept across her top lip and he nipped on her bottom one, she opened to him on a gasp and his tongue took immediate advantage.

The taste here was even more addictive than the taste of her lips. When her tongue tangled with his, he felt the jolt of desire rocket through his body, his dick jumping to attention, pressing solidly against the zipper of his jeans.

He felt like he was a kid, experiencing the first thrills of desire. He hadn't been a kid in more decades than he cared to remember, but he knew, with this woman, the feelings of discovery were only getting stronger.

She sighed softly into his mouth and wrapped her arms around his neck, drawing him closer. That sent his pulse rocketing like he'd just ridden the rapids and survived.

Everything zeroed in on three pleasure points.

Tongue to tongue.

Never had the tip of his tongue felt so sensitive. It wasn't a pain, but a pleasure so intense it flooded the rest of his senses.

He could taste her breath, mint with a hint of spring. His nostrils flared as if the taste of her was imprinting itself through his sinuses into his lungs. Her eyes, beautiful blue, deepened by her tears, were like he had dived below the surface of the lake. If he was going to drown, he'd do so willingly as long as he looked at her while it happened.

Chest to chest.

He could feel the weight of her breasts against his chest as they moved closer. Her nipples were buds of desire and he ached to take them into his hands, run his thumbs over them and bring them to his mouth to suckle.

Through their clothes, he felt his heart racing and knew, even though it didn't make sense that hers was echoing his, beat for beat.

Groin to pelvis.

She was sitting across his lap and his dick was pulsing like a stallion waiting for his mare. When she moved, getting closer to him, he wondered if he was going to explode right there in his jeans.

It would have been embarrassing if it weren't for the mewling sounds she was making deep in her throat. He knew she wanted more just as much as he did.

Finally, he eased his mouth away and touched his forehead to hers. His breathing was ragged and sounded like a rushing train in his ears. When her breath stuttered in and then out, he smiled and kissed her gently.

"Whew," she breathed it softly.

He grinned. "Whew is right. I didn't know how else to stop your crying. I was afraid you were getting hysterical."

She put her hand over her heart and took deep breaths. He felt his grin growing even larger. Of course, the grin was hiding the fact he'd nearly come in his jeans.

"Well, thanks. That's certainly a better method than shaking or slapping me," she said, with a smile.

"My pleasure, ma'am." He tipped his head and smiled. "Believe me, it was my pleasure."

As if realizing she was still sitting on his lap, she scooted away. He almost grabbed her and held her in place, but figured that would be pushing things a bit too far.

"Sorry about that," she said. "I don't usually fall apart like that. I just wasn't expecting it to be quite the fixer-upper that it is."

"No problem," he replied. *Now.* He should make his offer now. Instead he said, "I guess I'd better get going. I've got another job, then I'll go back to the office and get all the figures down."

He pushed a strand of her hair that was falling over her eyes back behind her ear. It was soft, like white gold, and he had a vivid mental picture of that hair draped across his hips as she worked her mouth over him. He felt like he was about to burst from need, but he wasn't going to do anything else. Not when she was still so vulnerable. He just wasn't that kind of man.

"Maybe it won't be as bad as I guessed. I'll pick you up at your hotel and we can have dinner and go over them. There's a nice place over in Lewiston."

Helen shook her head, swiped away the tears drying on her cheeks and replied, "I'm staying here. I figured it's a house, why pay for a motel, especially since the nearest one is in Lewiston and that's five miles away."

Bert frowned. "You're staying here?"

"Yes. It's my house."

"You don't have any furniture," he said.

"I know. I have a sleeping bag and an inflatable mattress in the car. The movers should be here tomorrow or the next day, although if it's as bad as you think, I probably should put most of my stuff in storage."

He rubbed a hand over his face, biting back his protest. She was right. It was her house. Temporarily. If she was already upset and they'd just started looking at what it was going to cost, she probably wasn't going to even last the week. With patience, he'd probably be able to get the house for a reasonable price.

"Well, okay. I'll stop by tomorrow with the final estimate. How's that?"

"That'll be fine," Helen said. "Thank you again for taking the time to come here today. I'll look forward talking with you tomorrow."

She turned, walked back to her car and opened the trunk.

He got in his truck and started down the road. He couldn't help looking in his rear view mirrors and watching the way she started unloading items, then carrying them to the house. Damn, he could tell by the way she was holding her shoulders and back that she was probably still crying.

Not my problem, he reminded himself. His goal hadn't changed since early this morning. Even if he did admire not only the way she looked, but the way she took things on that soft chin of hers.

He forced his attention back to the road in front of him ignoring the voice inside imploring for another look.

CHAPTER 2

Helen was happy when she got the stove to light on the first try. It was a gas stove, but was one that the pilot had to be lit with each use. She had followed the directions from the gas company exactly and was pleased when she got the clear blue flame. As she heated her soup, she decided that, although it was a simple supper, it was memorable because it was the first in her new home.

As the soup heated, she looked around her. She had two options the way she saw it. She could hope Bert's estimates were off, way off, on the high side. If that was the case, perhaps she would still be able to do it if she sold her car. It was new and had only the miles driven from Manhattan to western New York on it. She had never needed her own car while living in the city. Perhaps she could get back most of the money she'd spent on it.

The second option was she could postpone the opening of the bed and breakfast until she earned more money. Ramon had been right when he'd said she was a good cook. She was. Lewiston was five miles away and, although it was small, Bert had mentioned there was a nice restaurant there. Summer was almost here, so perhaps the restaurant hadn't hired all their seasonal help. If they didn't need a chef, she could always wait tables.

The one option she absolutely wouldn't consider was going back to the city. This was her home now. She would make it here or bust.

Her soup was steaming and she reached to turn the eye off. At that moment, she heard a strange sound and then the lights flashed brightly once before she was plunged into total darkness.

"Shit," she said, groping to try and find her way around the boxes she'd left on the kitchen floor. When she stubbed her toe against one, she cursed again.

Then, still stumbling around in the dark, she started when she heard a loud pounding on her front door.

"Helen, Helen?" Bert called. "Are you okay?"

Helen had feared her electricity wouldn't last so she'd taken the precaution of getting her flashlight out of her car. Her hand felt along the counter top until she found it and turned it on. She sighed. Now at least she could see and wouldn't be tripping all over everything just to get to the door.

The pounding continued.

"I'm coming," she called, as she hurried down the hallway. She opened the door and found him standing on her porch, a large bag in his hand. She could smell something delicious and, for a moment, she didn't know if it was the hot food in his hand or simply the man.

"Hi," she said. "I'm sorry. You caught me at a bad time. I just was making some soup and the power went out."

"Oh, well, if you're making soup, I guess you don't want this." He held up his bag.

She flashed the light on it and saw the bag was white and had a name stamped on it. She sniffed again.

"Whatever that is, it smells much better than soup," she said.

"Well, hope you don't mind, but I just thought I'd bring you some food. I didn't know if you had any groceries here or not."

"Thanks!" She opened the door wide for him to come in. "I had a few canned goods I brought from New York, but definitely nothing like this. It smells terrific by the way."

"I think you'll like it. It's a small, family-owned place in town. It's nothing fancy, but they do a good job."

"It smells great." She paused. "The place isn't really ready for entertaining."

He smiled. "Not to worry. I'm your contractor. I'm prepared to handle whatever crops up." He reached into the jacket of his brown leather bomber jacket and pulled out a pair of thick candles.

Helen laughed. "I can see that. Well, let's go back to the kitchen. I'm starving."

She turned and headed for the kitchen, with him following. She felt warm all over and knew his eyes were on her. It was thrilling and a little disconcerting. After the way they'd kissed, she really didn't know how to react.

First it was embarrassing to have broken down that way in front of someone she didn't know. It was even stranger to have had such an intense and immediate flair of attraction. Helen wasn't a naïve young woman. She'd been in love with her share of princes and frogs. Never, though, had she experienced the level of immediacy she did with Bert in a single kiss.

She also wasn't sure if she wanted to take it to the next step. The last time she'd mixed business with pleasure it'd turned out badly. This time, with her life savings already invested in this place, she wouldn't be able to leave town along with the relationship.

The final issue was trust. She didn't know Bert, so should she trust him?

In the final analysis, though, Helen decided she wasn't going to obsess about it. This was her home and a gorgeous, attractive man had brought her dinner to celebrate her first night here. She was just going to relax, let things develop naturally and enjoy the ride.

*   *   *

Bert followed Helen through the house. Even in the dark, the view in front of him was excellent. The boys in the testosterone band had started jumping out in song the moment she'd opened the door. In fact, they were beating a drumbeat that getting down to business right in the entry hall would be a huge hit.

But his mamma hadn't pounded manners into him for nothing. He also had a feeling that, no matter what, they were going to get to the important stuff before the night was done. Ever since he'd kissed her, he hadn't been able to get Helen off his mind. He thought about the estimates he had in his pocket. One was honest, a true estimate of what it would cost to completely renovate this house.

The other... Well, he wasn't going to think about the other estimate. He didn't know why he'd even taken the time to do it. It certainly didn't make any sense why he'd put it in his pocket along with the real one. He wouldn't, couldn't think about either estimate, though. Not now.

Now he wanted to find out more about the woman who'd spent her life savings on a wreck of a house. He had to find out why this was so important to her.

They reached her kitchen and he could see from the lighter and darker shades of black that she had a few boxes on the counters and floors.

"Do you want to eat in here?" he asked.

"No," she said. "It's very dark on this side of the house. I thought it'd be better to eat in the parlor. We'll have to eat on the floor, but with those big windows on the front, it's a bit lighter than in here. That's where I was planning to have my soup."

He nodded his head, then realized she couldn't see the movement. "Okay, I'll head back in there."

"Wait a minute. I have some silverware and plates. I also have some more candles that I dug out before I started cooking. I didn't want to count on the electricity holding up."

"Smart lady. I don't want this stuff to get cold, but after we eat, I can head down in the basement and check things out. Maybe I can get the electricity back on for a while at least."

"Oh, that would be wonderful," she said. "Are you an electrician as well as a contractor?"

"Oh, I'm a jack of all trades. Electrician, plumber, roofer, carpenter—you name it and on some job site somewhere I've had to fill the bill."

She panned her light over the counter and he clearly saw a box of matches and several candles of all sizes lined along the counter. She quickly started lighting them one after another. In no time, the room was highlighted with a soft, romantic, aromatic glow.

They transferred everything from the kitchen to the parlor. He groaned inwardly when they got there.

It was just as she'd said. She had her air mattress and sleeping bag open on the floor. She must have cleaned the front windows because the moonlight shone in a brilliant wide streak across the middle of the room, highlighting the bed. She started placing the candles in a circle at the edges of the moonlight, extending the light further and bringing warmth to the moonlight. At least it seemed very warm in the room to him.

She was moving like a whirlwind, making return trips to the kitchen, bringing silverware and plates with her, along with two glasses. When he saw them in her hands, he laughed. They were simple plastic cups like one would get for free with the purchase of a large convenience store drink.

"Sorry." She grinned when she saw him looking at the cups in her hands. "Most of my dinnerware is being shipped. But it was a long drive from Manhattan. I washed these, though."

"Not a problem. I'm a bachelor. That's the only kind of cups I had in my apartment for the first five years until my mother and sister ganged up on me."

She smiled in return. "Well, let's get settled. I'm starving."

"Me too," he replied. *But not just for the scampi.*

So they settled on her bed and dug into the containers of food he'd brought. She talked to him while they ate about her life in the hotel business and her dreams for the future. While she talked, he listened and watched. And wanted.

"Aren't you hungry?" she asked, when she realized he'd stopped eating.

"Yes," he replied. "For you."

He set his untouched plate aside and took her plate and silverware from her. Then he moved over to her.

Sitting in front of her, his legs spread out on either side of her, he pulled her into his embrace.

"After our kiss this afternoon, all I've thought about is having you," he said. "Please tell me to go. Or stay. Don't keep me waiting any longer."

She was silent and for a heartbeat, Bert thought she was going to send him packing. When she smiled slowly, he knew it was going to be okay.

*   *   *

God, she was babbling. He probably thought she was the biggest dope in the world.

She couldn't help it. She was excited. Beyond excited, she was giddy. When she'd opened the door and found him standing on her sagging porch with hot food in his hands, every part of her had melted.

After Ramon, Helen had told herself she was giving up on men. She didn't need one, she didn't want one. She had a flare of hope that Bert was different. The way he'd comforted her earlier this afternoon had been more than gentle, it had been spectacular.

As she had unloaded her car and tried to come up with a plan to make her dream come true, she'd been unable to get the taste of him, the feel of his strong shoulders and well defined chest under her hands out of her mind. A small bud of hope had formed in her heart. When he'd returned tonight, that bud had unfurled into a full bloom.

Now he was looking at her with so much need and desire in his eyes that she was overwhelmed. He was asking, not taking. There was no way she was going to turn him down.

She smiled at him and knew he could see her answer there. He pulled her across the short expanse of her bed and into his arms. She wrapped herself around him, legs around his waist and arms around his neck, holding on for the ride.

He started to kiss her. Helen sank into it. This man was, without a doubt, the best kisser she'd ever known. She didn't know if he was as good with his hands as he was his lips, but if he was, he'd be worth every penny he asked. But he was deadly with his lips.

He took his time, like tasting her mouth was the only thing he had in mind. He licked and supped at her bottom lip, making it an erogenous zone she never knew existed. His lips caressed in this half kiss that had her hungry for more, needy for her top lip to be included in the sensation. When he switched his attention higher and treated it to the same loving as he'd given her bottom lip, she nearly jumped out of her skin.

Finally, when she couldn't take any more of the teasing, she put her hands in his hair and held his mouth in place so hers could plunder.

Sharing breath had never been this exciting, not even that afternoon. Then had been about comfort and desire, but now was about need and greed.

Instinctively she knew he was just as needy and greedy as she was. Finally, they pulled apart. She removed her clothes and he did the same. They were kneeling on the mattress in their underwear.

"You're beautiful," he breathed.

She shook her head negatively. "No, I'm not, but thank you for saying so."

He placed two fingers over her lips stilling her words. Slowly he moved them lower, pulling on her full bottom lip, separating it from the upper, holding it down. Her tongue snuck out and laved at his fingers. His eyes widened with a renewed flare of desire. With fingers holding her lips apart, he began kissing her again.

Helen's breath caught and stuttered out on a sigh of overpowering need and desire.

After long moments, he separated them slightly. Helen licked her lips, missing the taste and feel of him against her, keeping her eyes closed to hold the memory.

But sounds soon filtered through her consciousness. It sounded like he was rustling paper.

She opened her eyes and heard him whisper, "No, keep them closed. I have a surprise."

So she closed them and stayed kneeling on the mattress. A few seconds later she felt something cool and deliciously sweet rub gently against her lips. Full, sweet, delicious cherries.

"Yum," she said, licking the juice from her lips and opening her eyes. He was holding a whole, deep red cherry just above her lips.

"They do a special cherries jubilee at the restaurant in Lewiston," he said. "This is my version."

He rubbed the cherry over her lips again and then put it in his mouth, lowering it until she had a choice. Eat the cherry or him.

She moved forward and nipped her teeth lightly into the small fruit. The taste of it exploded in her mouth, along with juice that was infused with brandy. Before she could recover from that delight settling over her tongue and taste buds, he set his mouth on top of hers, sharing the cherry and more with her.

The brandy moved down her throat and through her stomach like it was a wonderful fire. The kiss spun her out of control and suddenly she was wild for him, more than just his lips, tongue and teeth.

She pushed him so that he was on his back on the mattress. She worked his jockeys off his hips and down his legs. The sight of his wonderful full cock glittering in the candle light, with just a touch of his essence at its tip made her delirious. She had to have those strong nine inches as deep inside her as possible. She tore her panties and bra off, then settled her hips astride him, lowering herself until the head of him was just inside her pussy lips.

God, he was so big, so hot, so hard. She bit down on her bottom lip and slid another inch lower. It took all her control not to take him all in one shove, but she knew as good as it was now, it would only get better if she could only make it last longer.

So instead of impaling herself on him like her body and heart were demanding, she withdrew a bit and then took the head a little deeper.

The nerves just inside her pussy were throbbing with need. Her clit was pulsating with greed, wanting more.

She was wet, slippery wet with his moisture and hers mixing and they hadn't even gotten to the good part.

"Helen, God, please stop. I've got protection. Let me..." He trailed off as she took another inch of him.

He was right. She needed protection, but she was beyond that. She didn't want to stop. She wanted everything he had to give.

"I have an IUD," she gasped. "Oh, God, please tell me you don't have anything."

"God, no," he grunted. "Healthy as a horse." The last word trailed off as she slid down another inch, or perhaps two.

The head of him was teasing her inner lips. As she raised up again, he slid his hands down her body and managed to insert his index finger, palm up toward her tummy, reaching her G spot. God, with the size of his dick and his finger, Helen didn't know if she could take it, she was so filled. But after a moment, her muscles stretched and accommodated it.

When he applied the perfect amount of pressure Helen felt her clit swelling even more.

"Come for me, baby," he said. "Come now."

His words were all she needed. She lowered herself down his full length, taking him to the hilt at the same time he pressed again hard on her spot.

Helen shattered into pieces and felt the quakes of his body as his eruption flowed into her.

Moments, or perhaps hours later, Helen raised her head from where she was resting it against Bert's sweaty chest and looked at him. The candles threw interesting shadows across the planes and angles of his relaxed face. He was handsome and so dear to her already. She raised her hand and traced her fingertips across his eyebrows, touching the laugh lines that fanned out from their corners, then continued down his nose, with its small bump along the ridge. She wondered how and when it had been broken. He didn't open his eyes, but she could tell he was awake. His breathing changed just a bit and she felt the way his shaft, which had softened a bit after his first release, expanded inside her.

She smiled to herself. Her contractor man seemed to be about ready for round two. She definitely was ready.

She looked around. One of the candles flared as the flame dipped into the melted wax and she saw the container with the cherries to her left. She stretched and managed to pull it to her.

Her movement caused him to raise his eyebrow and one eye to pop open.

"Woman, I'll have you know I'm not an eighteen-year-old," he growled.

She risked a look upward and saw the glimmer of humor in his eyes.

"Old man, are you? Well, I'm a middle-aged woman. You know

what they say about us, don't you?"

He groaned. Now she definitely heard the humor.

"I'm at the prime of my sexual life," she continued. "Now, you just lay back and rest. I'll do all the work. I promise you'll keep up. Then again, if you can't, I promise you'll go with a smile on your face."

His laugh started low and deep in his belly. Helen took that as a sign and dipped her hand in the cooling cherries and their sauce. She traced her way down his rock hard six pack of abs, outlined his belly button, then moved lower, stopping just short of the thrusting evidence of his recovery.

She started licking where she'd left the cherries, using the flat of her tongue and just a few slight nips from her teeth. Her aim wasn't to mark him, just to let him know she was enjoying the taste of cherries and Bert. When she reached his belly button, she played there, paying particular attention to the rim and then dipping her tongue deep inside, erasing all traces of sweetness. It was a preparatory action for what she had in mind.

Finally she raised her mouth from his stomach and reached for more cherries.

His erection was huge. It was quivering as if he hadn't shot his load just minutes before.

"Oh, my," she said. "It looks like you're a bit uncomfortable there."

She looked up, wanting to watch his face as she pleasured him. Keeping her eyes on his face, she began covering his dick with the cherries and juice.

When it was covered to her satisfaction, she smiled and said, "Now, that's *my* idea of Cherries Jubilee."

She started slow, even though she was shaking with the need to swallow him whole. He was quivering as well and the sense of power that washed over her was fulfilling. To think she could make this beautiful, special man want her so much was thrilling.

In the past she'd been hesitant to experiment sexually. She didn't want to do something her lovers may not like. She didn't feel that way with Bert. Maybe it was because of her age. Or perhaps it was the way the approval was evident in his eyes, face and even the way his body was responding.

Whatever the reason, Helen gave head like she'd never given it before. There was no part of his genitals that were untouchable.

Her tongue was nothing more than a utensil for her pleasure and his. Her hands seemed to know the exact spots that made him jump and moan with ecstasy.

When finally she cleaned the last of the sugary cherry mixture from his throbbing cock, she licked one final time around the slit and then took his full length into her mouth.

"God, Helen," he moaned, his fist gripping her hair, holding her in place. "If I don't thrust, I'll die."

Helen relaxed her throat muscles and opened her mouth wider. She could still smell the cherries and him. She didn't know if she could take him as deeply as he probably wanted to go, but she decided she'd do her best.

She removed her mouth from him for a moment, took a deep breath and took him again.

Her descent was the affirmative he needed. As she lowered her mouth, he thrust his hips off the mattress. It only took two thrusts for him to release his seed with a shout of completion.

As she lay in his arms a few moments later, Helen knew the look on her face had to be that of a cat who'd just eaten a canary. She felt powerful and womanly, especially since, with her hand resting on his chest, she could feel the way his heart was still racing.

"Damn, woman, that near killed me," he finally said.

She raised her head and smiled.

"Really? Poor baby," she cooed. "I promise I won't do it again. At least for an hour or two."

He grinned in return.

"That should be about right." He slid out of her embrace and stretched out with his head toward her feet. "Especially for what I have in mind for you."

Helen held her breath as he went to work on her outer lips. His breath and tongue were soft, warm and patient. She was still pretty aroused, but he apparently wanted to make sure he didn't miss a single spot. By the time he flipped her over onto her stomach and stroked his tongue in the hollow between her cheeks, she was begging to be filled with him.

"You even taste good here," he murmured. "Are you ready for me to fuck you?"

"God, yes, Bert," she cried.

He thrust in to the hilt and she could feel the way his testicles slapped against her. He was so huge she thought he was going to come out her throat. She honestly didn't care and she told him so when she begged him for a release.

"Please, Bert, make me come now," she cried.

With his hands on her hips, holding her in place for his thrusts, he pounded into her. "Touch your clit," he groaned. "God, come for me."

She shook her head. She couldn't move. Every nerve and muscle in her body was desperate for his domination. She was so close to the most amazing peak she almost blacked out. It didn't seem possible, but it felt as if he grew larger inside her, her nerves rasping with a delight near to pain.

"Bert, hurry," she panted.

"No. Don't want it to end." His voice sounded almost delirious.

Helen didn't know how much more she could take. It was like every nerve in her body had moved to the point where her pussy and his cock merged and they were being pulled from beneath the skin so they were right on top, meeting each rasp, each thrust, each parry.

Finally she broke into a million glittering, tiny pieces. She heard his shout of satisfaction at the same moment she felt his waves of come hitting the walls of her uterus.

He collapsed against her back and his weight caused her knees to buckle so that she was laying on her stomach on the mattress.

She could feel his hot, lovely imprint on every inch of her. She smiled at the thought as she drifted off to sleep.

CHAPTER 3

Helen was straightening up the parlor a long while later. Bert was down in her basement trying to get her electricity back on. She knew it was silly, but she hoped he was unsuccessful. *At least for the rest of the night.*

She looked around at the melting candles, some still going strong, some gutted, and knew she'd never be able to walk into this room without remembering the sensational way she'd spent her first night here.

At that moment, the lights flashed on. She smiled as she continued to pick up the remains of their dinner. She was rejuvenated. She knew no matter what happened she had made the right decision moving here.

She could hear his footsteps as he came up the steps at the end of the hall. It was then she noticed the folded paper was resting just inside the bag that had carried their food. It didn't look like a receipt. It looked like an invoice.

She bent to pick up the bag as she heard him say as he came into the room, "It was just a minor problem. You blew the main fuse. I had a couple in the truck so I just had to screw the new one in. That should hold it for a bit. I'd certainly make the electrician the first order of business…"

He trailed off as he saw her standing there and looking at the paper in her hand.

"What's this?" she asked. She heard a roaring noise in her ears. It was as if time was standing still.

"It's my offer to buy this place," he replied evenly.

"Buy it?" The sex must have short-circuited her brain because she was hearing his words, but they weren't making any sense. "Why would I want to sell it? I just bought it. Why would you want to buy it?"

"Because it's more than you can handle." As he spoke he moved further into the room.

Helen held her ground, but she felt like running. That didn't make sense.

"Because you've never owned your own home and this is more than a fixer-upper. This is a fixer-nightmare."

Helen blinked. "But not for you?"

"No…it's what I do. I was going to talk to you about it at dinner, but we got sidetracked. I'll pay you what you paid for it, even though it's too much."

"How do you know what I paid?"

"Because when you paid the asking price, you bought it out from under me. They had my offer on the table. If you hadn't bought it, they were going to sell it to me. But that doesn't matter. What matters is that, with what I'll pay you, you can get you a really nice modern house in Lewiston or Youngstown. It'll be a house you can handle."

Helen felt the tears backing up and blinked to keep them from falling. "Is that what this"—she waved her hand, encompassing the bed, the remains of their dinner, the sex—"was all about? You were trying to get me to sell?"

"Yes. No." He sighed. "That was my plan when I came here this afternoon. I was going to do everything to talk you into selling."

She opened her mouth to respond, but, for some reason, her brain had short-circuited and she couldn't find the words she wanted to say.

He continued speaking before she could say a word. "But that plan changed when I met you. I couldn't do what I'd planned. So I came back tonight with another plan."

Now she found her voice. "What plan? Seduce me into giving you the house?"

She started to walk away, and where she was going she didn't know.

He grabbed her hand. "No. No, the seduction has nothing to do with the house. It's because you make me feel alive. Alive in a way I didn't think was possible at this point."

She looked at him. She prayed she was hiding the bloom of hope rising in her heart with skepticism on her face. "Are you telling me you fell in love at first sight?"

Now he looked even more frustrated. There was something else in his eyes as well. The hope in her heart grew stronger.

"I don't know. Before meeting you, I didn't think love at first sight was possible. Now I just don't know." He ran his hand again through his hair. "Look, I don't know if what we have will last. I think it will. It feels much stronger than anything I've felt before."

Helen released the breath she hadn't realized she was holding. "So what do you want, Bert?"

"Look, I want us to have a chance to see if this"—he opened his arms to everything that had happened between them—"will last. I want us to have a chance."

She nodded, trying to stay calm, when her insides were jumping up and down in glee.

"What about the house? You want it and you obviously have the ability and the money to fix it. Where does it fit in?"

He sighed. "Please, can we sit and talk?"

"There?" She pointed to the mattress, which was currently the only place to sit in the house.

His eyes brightened and he smiled ruefully. "I guess you're right. I already want to be with you again so bad I ache. Considering I've already done it with you more than I did it in a month before we met, I don't know if I'm able this soon."

Helen laughed. "I know what you mean. I always thought I was just a little frigid, if you want the truth."

He smiled. "Frigid? I don't think so. In fact, if you were any hotter you'd have burned me alive."

She knew he was telling the truth. His body and eyes weren't lying.

"Do you want to go somewhere that actually has chairs to talk?" she asked.

"No, we can do it here. What I'd like is to propose a partnership."

She frowned. This wasn't something she'd been expecting. Not even close. "I know it's silly wanting to turn this place into a bed and breakfast, but this is my dream. Haven't you ever had a dream?"

"Actually, yes. This house is my dream as well. I wanted to fix it right. I can do most of the work myself. I wanted to put mahogany floors in here. I wanted to change the door and put stained glass on top of the front, in a rainbow shape. I wanted to make this a showplace. Something people would come from all over the region to see."

"Oh. Your dream sounds beautiful." She felt her hopes deflating. His dream sounded so good and so expensive. She knew it was completely out of her price range. But she could also see it just as he described. The house would be something special. It would be magnificent. In a startling moment of clarity, she realized he could make his dream a reality. Her dream would never become real. "And so much more worthy than mine."

"Hey, don't say that." He put his hands on her shoulders and forced her to look at him. "You have a right to your dreams. Just like I have a right to mine."

She bit her bottom lip. He leaned forward and kissed her.

"It's just a shame we can't somehow put the two together."

She frowned. An idea was blooming. He'd suggested a partnership. Would he want to take that further?

"You want to make this house a showplace," she spoke slowly. "I want to open up a bed and breakfast. Wouldn't you think a showplace bed and breakfast would be even better than an ordinary one?"

He opened his mouth and said nothing for a few moments. "Me and you running this place?" he asked.

"Partners?" She held out her hand to him.

He took it and brought it to his lips.

"Partners," he agreed.

"I've always been a sucker for a happy ending," she replied before wrapping her arms around his neck and hugging him close.

"So, what do you say about christening the master bedroom," he said against her lips.

"I don't know," she replied. "I have it on good authority the place isn't habitable."

"Authority nothing," he said as he led her back over to her mattress. "We don't need electricity because, lady, you provide enough to light up the entire county."

"Only with you, sir. Only for you." She said on a laugh that quickly turned to a groan.

*   *   *

NOW OPEN
Dreams do come true! Come share ours!
Authentic, refurbished Victorian-era bed and breakfast on the shores of Lake Ontario now taking reservations. Reasonable rates and great food. Million-dollar view will rejuvenate and inspire.
Call 888-888-8888 for more information.

HERO ADRIFT

"I shall sell life dearly to an enemy of my country,
but give it freely to rescue those in peril.
With God's help, I shall endeavor to be one of His noblest Works…"

From the Creed of the
United States Coast Guardsman
(written by VADM Harry G. Hamlet)

CHAPTER 1

"Okay everyone, stay calm!" Abby called. "I'm sure someone will be here to help us as soon as possible."

She turned quickly to her teacher's assistant, a young man who looked almost as frightened as the nineteen six-year-olds who made up her class. They were part of a large group of first-graders taking a tour on a sightseeing boat that traversed the Niagara River between Buffalo and Niagara Falls. With parents and children, there were nearly one hundred people on the boat called the *Niagara Belle,* and they were currently dead in the water.

Abby tried to smile reassuringly again. Things were not looking good.

Abby's class was from the Buffalo School. Things had been going extremely smooth on this late-spring sightseeing trip and the children had been having a great time, in addition to learning a lot about the history of the great river and the Erie Canal. In fact, things had been going so well Abby had finally relaxed. But that's what she got for letting her guard down. Now things were looking bleak. She could feel her throat tighten and her panic begin to rise.

The water of the Niagara that had looked calm and peaceful at the start of the tour now looked dark and dangerous. The wind had picked up and was whipping in off Lake Erie, bringing with it the cold bite of winter still lingering over western New York and lake waters that hadn't begun to warm for the summer. Worse, there was a large black cloud coming in from the west. It appeared to Abby as if it was being pushed by a rocket on a collision course with them.

Add to all this the danger of the river and the dead tour boat...her captain apparently suffering a heart attack. Abby sucked in a deep breath. Well, it wouldn't do to panic. She had to be strong and self-assured or her children would pick up on her fears.

"Okay, kids, everyone find your buddy and line up in a straight line behind Mr. Stella," she called. "Let's let the crew and Dr. Bailey do their work."

Dr. Bailey and one of the chaperones, who was a nurse, were working feverishly on the captain. The boat had an emergency medical kit and Abby knew that calls had already been made to 911. In fact, as she looked out over the bow, she could see a large white-and-red boat coming to them. She smiled again. *Everything's going to be fine.*

She wouldn't even think about the fact it seemed as if the *Belle* was drifting closer and closer to the large International Railroad Bridge that crossed the Niagara from Buffalo's Black Rock neighborhood to Fort Erie, Ontario. What could happen? Just because the bridge had been built in 1870 and was still used today, surely a ninety-foot long cruise and tour boat built in the 1990s could handle ramming into the bridge supports. *Right?*

Abby closed her eyes as another wave of panic threatened to overcome her. She'd put that right out of her mind. That just left room for the thought of what would happen if a bridge meant to carry the weight of freight trains collapsed on top of their relatively modern boat.

"Look, Ms. Smithton. The Coast Guard is coming," one of the children cried.

Abby looked back out over the bow and could now make out the markings on the white boat. The child was right. It was the Coast Guard. And Abby could see there were other boats speeding to their rescue as well. Abby smiled, starting to really relax. "Yes, I see. I told you there was nothing to worry about. Now hurry up and find your buddy."

Abby refused to think about how they were going to get everyone off the *Niagara Belle* and onto the other boats. Well, maybe they'd just tow the *Belle* and her passengers back to shore. There probably wouldn't be any danger of anyone having to step over the water. At any rate, Abby knew the Coast Guard and all the other rescue teams were the experts. She'd let them handle it.

She wasn't afraid of water...she just didn't like the fact she couldn't see the bottom. She wouldn't think about what it would be like stepping across a chasm between two heaving decks. It probably wouldn't even come to that.

"Everyone, here I am," called John Stella, her teacher's aide.

Some kids were scurrying to obey, while a few others lingered at the rail. Abby went over to hurry them along.

She felt a tug on the bottom of her blouse and looked down at the excited face of Billy Borrelli.

"Ms. Smithton, do you think the Coast Guard will ram us?" he asked with a mixture of fear and excitement on his cherubic face and in his voice.

"No, Billy, they will not ram us," she said firmly.

"Oh." He looked a bit crestfallen. "Well, it could happen."

"Only on a computer game," she replied. "Now hurry up and find your buddy and get in line. We want to be able to do everything the Coast Guard tells us when they get on board, okay?"

Billy nodded and took one last long look at the boats drawing up to them.

Another child called her name and she turned away, one thought in her mind—getting everyone safely off this boat and back on land.

* * *

The *U.S.S. Comfort* pulled aside the *Niagara Belle* and Petty Officer Oliver Robinson balanced his weight on the balls of his feet as the skipper, Lieutenant George Danheiser throttled back and sent the diesel engine of their forty-seven-foot Motor Life Boat into idle. The current on the Niagara River was fast, with wind whipping up around twenty knots causing whitecaps to swell. The *Belle* was being pulled closer and closer to the International Railway Bridge and no one wanted to see whether ship or bridge would win that battle. The destruction was one thing, the possible disruption of the commercial railway traffic between the United States and Canada another. In fact, Oliver looked over and saw a boat from the Canadian Coast Guard tearing up river, as well as support craft from the local law enforcement agencies.

The plan was to position the *Comfort* in front of the *Belle* and, using a tow line, keep her steady while they transferred the passengers to smaller crafts and returned them to land. Perhaps in normal situations, they would just leave the passengers aboard and tow the *Belle* back to port. But this wasn't a normal situation. They had a report the *Belle's* captain had collapsed with a possible heart attack. They also had learned the *Belle* was hosting over a hundred elementary school students from the area. No one wanted to risk anything happening to the youngsters, so the decision had been made to take everyone off the *Belle,* just in case.

Search and rescue were the prime functions of the Coast Guard and one of the biggest reasons Oliver had signed up. Of course, since he'd been in, things had changed with the Guard taking on more and more responsibilities for law enforcement and homeland security.

But search and rescue had always held a special spot in Oliver's gut. It was the thing he'd miss most when he left the Guard.

This rescue was a little trickier than normal because of the children involved, but he also felt a little relieved. Oliver had just been transferred to Buffalo after spending eight months at Air Station Miami, where the duty was always exciting and hazardous. Buffalo normally wasn't quite so active, but with his shoulder still acting up after he had been shot on his last Miami op by the drug dealer they were trying to capture, Oliver could use a little light duty.

He turned his thoughts away from Miami. There was no use going over it again because thinking about that evening just pissed him off and he couldn't do anything to change what had happened. He also didn't need to have those thoughts in his mind when he was facing a rescue.

One thing Oliver had learned early in his CG career was to never take any rescue for granted and keep his mind one hundred percent on the job.

The *Comfort* was in place and Oliver saw the signal from Danheiser that things were ready. Seaman Joe Poreda stepped from the *Comfort* onto the *Belle,* temporary anchor in hand, and headed to the stern. He made quick work of securing the anchor and then tying off a couple of lead ropes as well, making sure the *Comfort* would help keep the *Belle* steady.

"Man overboard!"

The shout sent a chill down Oliver's back and he looked all around the *Belle.* He saw the flash of orange of a P.F.D., a personal floatation device, off the port side. God, it was a child.

Oliver knew the average water temperature of the Niagara River in the middle of May was 45.2 degrees. An adult would be exhausted swimming in that temperature in around thirty to forty minutes. Then there was the speed of the current and the real possibility the victim was injured and would drown even with the P.F.D.

But this was a child. That ratcheted things up quite a bit. He wouldn't have a child drown. Not on his watch.

In the time it took him to pull his protective waterproof headgear into place, another call rang overboard. "Man overboard times two!"

Damn. This simple rescue had gone to shit in an instant he thought as he flipped over the rail and headed for the first flash of orange he saw.

* * *

"Sixteen, seventeen, eighteen," Abby counted the children lined up. "Oh, God, who's missing?"

Frantically she looked at the faces of her children. ""Where's Billy?" she asked John.

"I don't know," he replied. "He was just there a minute ago. I saw you talking to him."

"He was worried about us getting rammed by the Coast Guard," Abby said. She was turning to her right and left, praying she'd find the little boy soon. The man overboard call came just as her gaze ricocheted out the boat and she saw the flash of orange over the left railing.

The Coast Guardsman was at the other end of the *Belle.* There was an Erie County sheriff's patrol boat on the left side and the students were standing on the right. She could see another boat racing to them from the Canadian coastline, but she wasn't certain if they'd reach them or if they could see Billy's orange life jacket and body. Abby knew Billy had only one chance. She bit back her fear at the thought of the cold, dark water coming over her head, but closed her eyes and jumped in. Billy was her responsibility. She didn't take that lightly.

For a second she was afraid she'd be pulled to the bottom—the bottom she couldn't see and certainly couldn't feel under her feet. But the life jacket she was wearing did its job and popped her to the surface. The water was cold—much, much colder than she'd expected for this time of the year. Abby's teeth begin chattering within seconds of being in the river. She couldn't imagine what Billy, who weighed maybe forty-five pounds versus her one hundred and twenty-five, was feeling. Abby put the cold out of her mind, however. She had only one thought—reaching Billy. Although the thick jacket made movement awkward and Abby wasn't the strongest swimmer in the world, she started kicking and stroking her way to where Billy was bobbing away from the *Belle* at an alarming rate.

Abby felt the combination of the strong current and the cold begin sapping her strength almost immediately. She had to reach Billy. She kept her eyes on him and yelled, "I'm coming, son."

Her words ended on a cough as the wind whipped what felt like a gallon of water into her open mouth, down her windpipe and into her lungs.

Abby heard shouts behind her and knew there were others coming to help. But she also saw the panic in Billy's eyes as she got closer to him. Although the life jacket was keeping his head above water, she could tell he was quickly losing the ability to stay afloat.

She finally reached him and wrapped him in her arms. "I'm here, darling. I'm here. Put your arms around my neck, okay?"

Billy nodded. She could see the tinge of blue around his lips from the cold and exhaustion and heard the rasp as he gasped for breath. Billy was asthmatic and she knew he was having an attack.

At that moment one rescuer reached them.

"Hurry," she said to the man. "He's having an asthma attack."

Their rescuer nodded and took Billy from her arms, then turned and swam to the back of the Coast Guard boat, which seemed closer than it had been before. There were a man and woman wearing Coast Guard uniforms and one of them was readying emergency equipment. She opened her mouth to repeat her warning about Billy's condition when the rescuer beat her to it.

"He's got asthma, according to his mother," the swimmer said as he handed Billy into the outstretched arms of a seaman leaning over the rescue boat. "I didn't see evidence of any head trauma, but I didn't check closely."

"His name is Billy," Abby called. She was paddling behind the rescuer, thinking it had looked so easy when he'd reached the boat with Billy. For her, it seemed as if the boat was getting farther away rather than closer. She was appalled at how much her strength had been sapped by the experience. Perhaps she should be actually going to the gym instead of just paying for the membership. "I'm not his mother. I'm his teacher. Please hurry."

A strong hand grabbed her wrist and pulled her the rest of the way through the water. Her muscles felt like they weighed a ton. Okay, she was definitely going to have to lay off the ice cream and hit the gym. Starting tomorrow. She looked at the puckered skin on her fingers. Check that. She'd hit the gym the day after because it was going to take at least forty-eight hours to thaw out. Wanting to at least do something for herself, Abby tried to grasp the rail, but her hands were so cold she couldn't feel the metal, and the material of her pants seemed to be wrapped around her legs like manacles, hampering her movements even more.

"Come on, lady, upsy daisy," her rescuer said.

His voice seemed right behind her ear and his breath sent a fresh wave of shivers down her back. He seemed so warm and solid behind her, it was a temptation to rest against him and let him handle everything.

The water really was colder than she expected. Had she read somewhere that hypothermia could cause delirium?

Then she felt his hand cup her bottom and knew cold could affect someone's mind because suddenly all she could think about was having that strong hand touch nothing but her flesh.

Before she could do much more than wonder at the thoughts rushing through her, she was shoved out of the water and over the rail onto the deck.

The next few minutes were a blur of activity for Abby. Someone threw a heavy blanket to her and she managed to wrap it around herself as she watched the crew working on Billy. They already had him hooked up on oxygen and were taking his vitals.

"His name is Billy Borrelli," she gasped, still trying to catch her breath. "His parents are William and Cheryl Borrelli. I believe his father works at the *Buffalo News*."

Even though no one responded to her information, she knew they heard it because they were relaying it to the emergency room with which they had established contact. Abby shivered but was happy when she saw the litter Billy was on being lifted and then passed onto another, smaller craft from the Erie County Sheriff's department. One of the Coast Guard crewmembers went as well and soon the boat powered up and sped away to the shore. Abby could see several rescue vehicles parked and ready to ferry any victims to the hospital.

Taking her first easy breath since she'd discovered Billy was overboard, Abby turned and met the icy-blue gaze of her hero. He was, without a doubt, the most gorgeous man she'd ever seen. His black hair, now visible since he'd removed his diving head gear, was damp and dark as midnight. His nose was long and sculpted like a Greek god's. There was a small, uneven bump midway along the bone, as if it had been broken at some point. His face was deeply tanned, not a tan she was used to seeing this early in the spring in Buffalo, so she guessed he'd recently moved here from somewhere southern and warm.

She had an instant vision of him and her lying side by side, the sand beneath their bodies not nearly as hot as the feel of his fingers running over her aroused flesh.

She shook her head. The cold water must have knocked more than a few circuits loose. Sure it had been a while since she'd had a boyfriend—okay, more like an eternity—but she didn't usually have an erotic fantasy while awake and facing a life-altering emergency.

She looked away from his face and noticed the rest of him, outlined perfectly in his wet suit. Oh, my, she thought.

His body was hard and leanly muscled as if he had been carved from stone. If his hair hadn't been so military short, he'd have been a dead ringer for the actor Eric Bana in the movie *Troy*. Abby felt like every speck of saliva in her mouth was drooling from her lips. She swallowed and tried to get her tongue to do something besides pant.

"Thank you for rescuing Billy and helping me." She finally managed to form coherent words.

"You're welcome. But, lady, that was an incredibly stupid thing to do. Don't ever jump in after somebody like that again. You could've both drowned."

"You're right. Thank you again for being there for us," she said.

*   *   *

Abby watched as her boat took her back ashore. Her hero and the other members of the *U.S.S. Comfort* were still onboard their boat. It looked as if the Coast Guard was going to tow the *Belle* back to shore. Probably to be inspected or whatever it was the Coast Guard did after incidents like this. She turned and looked at the shoreline. The deputy from the sheriff's department told her they would be returning her to the dock where the tour had started. She was glad. She needed to reassure the rest of the children she was fine, as well as make sure they were all returned safely to their parents.

After that, she would go to Children's Hospital, where Billy had been taken, to check on him and talk to his parents. She looked back over her shoulder. She really should forget all about her hero. She'd probably never see him again. Women like her didn't come in contact with heroes often, though, and she couldn't stop thinking about him. Nor could she pass up the chance to look at him one more time as the boat sped her further away from him. She just wished she knew his name.

*   *   *

Oliver cruised the narrow parking lot behind the apartment building looking for an empty spot. According to the guys at the station he was fortunate to have found an apartment with off-street parking because, when the snow started flying next winter, he'd be happy to get his car off the streets. He shivered a little and pulled the collar of his USCG-issue parka higher on his neck. The guys had said the worm had turned here weather-wise and that summer was around the corner. He didn't know about that. He felt like he was freezing and it was the middle of May. His last shift in Miami had been early April and it had already been a sultry eighty degrees. He bet it hadn't even reached fifty here today.

When he saw an opening a few feet ahead of him, he punched the accelerator and eased into the spot, with inches to spare. Well, Buffalo may not have been on his top ten garden duty spots for transfer six weeks ago, but he guessed it could've been worse. Here he'd only been on watch for four days and he had already had a rescue. Some of the Group Buffalo veterans predicted that, shortly after Memorial Day, things would really get hopping as all the recreational boaters would be out in force.

As he put the car into park and turned it off, he thought about the rescue yesterday. Truth told he had been a little shaky going into it. He hadn't really known how well his shoulder would hold up to the stress of rescue work. The surgeons had said all the major muscle masses in his shoulder and upper arms were healed, but he figured that was easy for them to say since they weren't the ones using them. Now he knew he could handle anything.

As he reached behind him for his seabag he felt a little pull and amended that thought. Well, maybe not anything. His thoughts returned to the round woman who'd showed more guts than brains when she'd jumped into the water after that little boy. The boy was fine. Oliver had checked with the hospital before leaving the station. He hadn't dropped by the hospital—he'd had more than enough of hospitals lately—but it was good to know the kid was fine. So was the woman.

He whistled softly thinking about her. Oh man, she was a package all right. After the too-thin bodies that seemed to be everywhere in Miami, this woman had been a sight for his hungry eyes. And, after taking the dive into a river, her figure had been clearly outlined in the pants and blouse she'd worn. He'd never seen a fully-clothed person who actually looked good wearing a regulation P.F.D., but this woman had been close. When he'd boosted her up on the deck of the *Comfort*, he'd had his hands full of the softest, roundest piece of ass he'd seen in years. Even now, nearly forty-eight hours after the incident, just thinking about it almost gave him a hard-on.

If that was the kind of action awaiting him here in Buffalo, he could see how this duty was going to be no hardship at all.

*   *   *

Abby opened her apartment door and stomped out into the entrance hall of her building. What a truly shitty forty-eight hours. First she got wet and cold trying to rescue one of her children, and now it seemed she was on the verge of losing her job.

One of the parents was threatening to sue the school district over the incident on the boat. It wasn't Billy's parents. They had been more than thankful and grateful for Abby's actions. Even after she told them that she didn't actually rescue Billy—the real hero was the dreamy Coast Guard swimmer—the Borrellis had insisted on playing up her part of the rescue.

That's what made the lawsuit threat so disheartening. The parents filing the suit claimed they hadn't given permission for their son to go on the trip, and neither had they signed a permission slip. Abby had double and triple-checked the sheets to make sure all the children had signed permission forms, but now those forms couldn't be found. Abby was uncertain if they were still on board the *Belle,* which was being held for investigation by the Coast Guard, or if they had fallen out of her trip folder on the bus.

The school board was worried other parents would be jumping on the litigation bandwagon, and Abby knew the board would be meeting tomorrow night in a closed session to discuss the issue. If she'd had a few more years' teaching experience, she could probably weather this storm. But she hadn't been tenured yet, so she didn't have much say in the whole thing.

It just wasn't fair. She was a great teacher and she loved her job. She'd just been trying to do what was right. She really needed a hero now, but she knew the likelihood of finding one was small. She'd had her brush with true bravery and she still didn't know his name.

She stepped across the small hall to where the building's mail boxes were and sighed. Maybe there was a way to at least learn her hero's name. What would it hurt to call the Coast Guard and see if they'd tell her who he was? She had her key in the lock when she felt and heard the swoosh of the outside door opening, followed by the inside foyer's door.

The man that came in was not one of regular neighbors. Perhaps her prayers would be answered after all.

It was her Coast Guard hero in the flesh, and he looked even better dry than he had wet. Abby tried to smile and hoped he wouldn't realize she was creaming her panties.

"It's you!" she said. She hoped he wouldn't think the grin she knew was on her face was sappy.

He stood strong, tall, proud and, Abby felt like she was two seconds away from being a puddle at his feet.

"Yes," he said. "I just got off my shift. We work four days on and four off."

Abby nodded. She felt she had to say something. But what could she say? She didn't think it would be a good idea to ask him to marry her. Not yet anyway.

"Do you live here?"

"I'm 1C," he said, shifting the duffle bag he was carrying and setting it on the floor. He was wearing a parka, which he unzipped now he was inside. She thought it weird to be wearing such a heavy coat in May. It reinforced her thought that his tan didn't look like he had been living here very long. "Moved in last week, but then I reported immediately to the station. This will be my first night actually staying here."

"Oh, 1C is right next to me. I'm 1B," she added.

He smiled and Abby felt her as if her insides were not melting now, but were molten lava rushing down the inside of her body like magma moves to the sea. "Now that's handy, isn't it? B being next to C and all."

"Yes. Welcome to the building then and thanks for rescuing us yesterday," she said, even as she thought she sounded like such a ditz. Heroes probably would be bored stiff within minutes with a ditz, so she needed to rally her thoughts and start acting like she had a clue.

She didn't want to seem too much like Lois Lane in the presence of Superman. Although, if Superman looked half as good as her hero, Abby could understand how Lois felt.

"Hey, you're welcome," he replied. "I called the hospital. They said the little boy is going to be fine."

"Yes." Abby smiled and started to relax. She could do this—have an intelligent conversation with a god and sound coherent. "Billy is going to be fine. Perfect in fact."

"That's good. We always worry when there are children involved."
He held out his hand. "By the way, I don't think we were ever
introduced. I'm Oliver."

She placed her hand inside his and felt like she was touching a live
wire as the heat from his contact raced up her arms, telegraphed itself
down the nerves of her spine and straight into her pussy.

She looked up into his beautiful, dark eyes and it was the same
body-engulfing feeling she'd just experienced when she'd dove into the
cold waters of the Niagara River after Billy. The biggest difference this
time was that she didn't feel one bit cold. This time she felt like she
was diving into a river of that molten lava burning through her blood.

"I'm Abby," she replied.

"Well, nice to officially met you, Abby. And even nicer to learn
we're neighbors." His smile lit up his eyes.

She felt his pull and knew she could easily stand there looking at
him for the rest of her life.

"Nice meeting you and welcome to the building," she said, finally
pulling her hand from his. She started to turn back to her door when he
stopped her.

"Hey, I know it's short notice, but I'm really not all that tired.
Would you like to go out for dinner or something?" he asked. "I mean I
only just moved to Buffalo, but I can probably find someplace around
here that's decent for dinner."

Abby smiled. "Well, since I'm a native, I can definitely recommend
a good place or two. Besides, I'd like to do something for you since
you came to the rescue with Billy."

"Aw, shucks, just doing my job, ma'am," Oliver said. "I'll let you
pick the place, but I insist on it being my treat."

Abby chewed on her bottom lip and thought quickly. She wasn't
sure if she should do this since they'd just met, but she needed a
change. Playing it safe hadn't gotten her anywhere except possibly out
of work, so she decided to wing it. Until the moment she'd jumped into
the river after Billy, she'd played it safe her entire life.

"Give me an hour and come over to my apartment. Deal?"

He smiled and it stole her breath again. "Deal, neighbor."

As she turned to head into her apartment, she heard the sound of a
soft whistle. Even if it wasn't safe, Abby had an idea it was going to be
a lot of fun.

*   *   *

Oliver finished shaving and whistled as some classic rock and roll played in the background. The first thing he'd done when he'd walked into his apartment was hook up his stereo. He'd left the rest of his stuff, what there was of it, in the boxes. The apartment was furnished, which was good because he didn't own any of his own furnishings. Besides, things like furniture slowed a guy down.

Who'd have thunk on his first night off in Buffalo he'd be going on a date with one of the hottest women he'd met in years. He'd been so tired after his shift that he'd turned down an offer to go with some of his boat crew members to their favorite watering hole. Once he'd walked into the building, though, and found out who his neighbor was, all thoughts of exhaustion had fled. Sleep and unpacking were the last priorities on his mind now. He was feeling ready to rock the night away.

He wondered where the sexy elementary school teacher would take him. It would probably be somewhere loaded with atmosphere, a place they could quietly get to know each other. He sighed. He could do quiet. Especially if this place had a small dance floor that would give him a chance to get her in his arms again.

He felt himself harden at that thought and looked down at the way his erection was already straining the fabric of his skivvies. He frowned. He probably should have never asked Little Miss Schoolteacher out. She had ivory trellises and forever-after written all over her. She was a woman who needed a hero, like those in a romance novel. She probably had a bookcase full of romances and dreamed of heroes every night.

Once, before Miami, he'd thought of himself as a hero. Now he knew better.

He frowned when he thought back to the discussion he'd had with the Group Commander that morning. At one point Oliver had been a poster Guardsman. *That was before Miami.* The commander had reminded him of what the Guard's motto, *Semper Paratus* meant. Always Ready. Though the official stance was they didn't want heroes, they wanted well-trained men and women ready to do a job and save lives. But the perception of the public, especially after well-publicized rescues during recent hurricanes, was that hero and USCG were synonymous.

Well, he wasn't ready for it any more. He was weary. He was tired. He just wasn't cut out of the hero cloth.

As for the other…well, he wasn't a forever kind of guy. In fact, he couldn't even say if he was a six-week kind of a guy.

He sighed and turned away from the mirror. He wouldn't think about what he saw in there now. He'd concentrate on having a good time with a woman. It didn't matter what she wanted in the future, as long as she understood he only came for the night.

*   *   *

The knock sounded on her door exactly one hour later. Abby smoothed down the line of her black mini skirt and tugged at the red Jacarda silk jacket. The jacket covered a barely-there tank top. Abby hoped she wouldn't have to worry about being cold for long, but just in case, she pulled her fall coat out of the closet, then took one last deep breath to calm herself. Tonight, she was determined to forget everything and just have fun!

She opened the door and smiled at her flesh and blood hero. "Hi. Right on time. Let's go."

CHAPTER 2

Oliver set his drink down and tried to keep from jumping over the table and climbing on Abby. She looked delectable. The restaurant she had directed him to was a place full of people dancing and talking, and she was the hottest looking woman there. Since they'd been here, he'd had to give several guys a back-off stare. All because the witchy outfit she was wearing nearly screamed, "Fuck me." Oliver glared at another guy leering at Abby. This was his demure elementary school teacher?

"Let's dance," he said, taking her hand in his.

He pulled her behind him and made a spot for them on the crowded floor. When he pulled her into his arms, she smiled up at him.

"I thought you'd never ask. If you'd kept quiet for ninety more seconds, I'd have dragged you out here myself."

"Well, if you hadn't worn that outfit that's driving every man in here insane, I wouldn't have had to spend the last hour protecting my turf," he replied.

Her head rested perfectly against his chest and her arms were entwined around his neck. He wrapped his arms around her waist and pulled her against his body. She was soft and her curves were like holding heaven in his arms. He knew she could feel the way his erection was growing, but he wasn't trying to hide it.

"Sorry," she said.

He could tell from the way her eyes glinted that she wasn't sorry at all.

"I don't usually dress like this. In fact, I never come here. But tonight I just felt like doing something dangerous."

"Ah. Well, I'm glad you allowed me to be part of it. I can do danger as long as you're involved." He moved his mouth so it hovered over her lips, letting her feel his words as well as hear them.

She shivered a bit and he hoped he was correctly reading the desire she was feeling by the way her body moved sinuously against his. He pulled her tighter against him and kissed her. He tried to keep it slow, sensuous, even though every inch of him was demanding hard and hot. She gasped and opened her lips, allowing him to sweep his tongue inside her mouth. He could taste the remnants of her dinner and the sweetness of the after-dinner cocktail she'd been sipping. When the tip of her tongue tangled with his, he forgot everything, including where they were and what they were doing.

Long moments later he finally came up for air and realized the music had stopped. Her lips were glistening, red and juicy like sweet cherries. It took all of his control not to swoop back in for another taste of heaven, but he didn't think getting arrested for public indecency his first night off in town would look good.

"Can we leave?" he asked instead, hearing the unsteady need in his voice.

"Yes."

He kept one of her hands in his as he led her back to their table. They picked up their coats and he threw some cash on the table to cover the bill and tip. He followed her from the restaurant and he looked up. The moon was so bright and the night sky was a perfect ink black. He could feel the bite of a chill in the air, but otherwise it was a beautiful night. The restaurant she had chosen was one that sat on a pier overlooking the Niagara River just north of where the *Belle* had been rescued. The wind had died and he could see the moonlight laying a blanket of white light across the glassy calm water.

"Well, it isn't Miami, but we like it," she said softly as she stood on the pier and looked at out the river and Lake Erie in the distance.

"Not being Miami is a good thing," he replied. The air had cooled his desire somewhat. He still wanted her, but he also wanted to spend some time in the welcome quiet of the pier after the frenetic party scene inside. He followed when she walked over to the rail and leaned against it. He stood behind her and placed one arm on either side of her. She leaned back against him and he felt a sense of something deeper than simple desire wash over him.

"Can you tell me what happened there?" she asked softly.

"What makes you think anything happened?" He was uncertain if he was ready to bare his soul.

She shrugged, the movement brushing her head against his chin. Her hair smelled fresh and was softer than the silk she wore beneath her coat. He moved his arms from the wooden railing and wrapped them around her waist, pulling her back until her spine rested against his chest.

"I don't know. It just sounded like it just now."

He sighed. "Let's just say I'd had enough of Miami, okay?"

She stiffened momentarily, then relaxed. "Sure. You know, the way the river looks now, it's hard to believe how much trouble we were in yesterday."

"Yes, and we just got you guys ashore when the storm rolled in. It was pretty nasty. I guess the weather is very unpredictable here," Oliver replied.

"Not usually at this time of year. We were their first tour of the season for the company."

"The tour company is probably going to face a huge fine. They're probably going to have to stop their tours for a while until all their boats are re-inspected."

Abby said, "Let's talk about something else. What do you think of this place?"

"The place is fine," he answered. "The company is better, though."

She relaxed again and he pulled her tighter against him. Even through her coat he could feel the way her hips nestled against his cock. The desire in his blood that had turned down to a simmer began to boil again.

He turned her around so she was facing him. She smiled up at him and he kissed her again, this one going to scorching immediately. When they finally separated, they were both breathing rapidly.

"Take me home, Oliver." The hot desire in her eyes inflamed him even more.

The short trip home seemed interminable to him, but finally they stood at her door, and the light from her front room, warm as it spilled out into the hallway, made her eyes glimmer like soft pools of jades. He couldn't remember the last time he had wanted a woman this quickly or this completely. He started to reach for her and pulled back his hand when he realized it was shaking with need.

"Well, good night," he said, needing some space before he lost all his sanity.

"Oh, no, not good night," she said She reached for the lapel of his jacket and pulled him inside her apartment. "You're not going to get away from me that easily. Not after driving me insane at the restaurant."

He saw the look in her eyes. It was all desire. She was right. They'd both gone too far to turn back.

She fused her lips with his as she backed them deeper into her apartment. Two sets of hands were frantic pulling off coats, then top layers of clothing.

He couldn't stop kissing her, which made finishing undressing a slow but sensual process. When he got her down to just the silk tank top and her panties, he broke the kiss to move his mouth over her breasts. Cupping them both in his hands, he stretched the fabric until it was taut over her rapidly hardening nipples. He plucked at them and smiled in delight at their response.

Yes, everything about this woman was just perfect, he thought as he moved back to her lips to send them both spinning again.

*   *   *

Abby felt the jolt of desire rage through her and set up an answering throbbing in her clit when he touched her breasts. Good Lord, he was like a fever in her blood with his intoxicating kisses and touches. When his hands moved back to her breasts and he plucked at her nipples, she felt her legs begin to quiver. She pushed his shirt—which she'd finished unbuttoning before he began his sensual assault on her breasts—off him and managed to unbuckle and unzip his pants.

She could see the outline of his erect cock through his white boxer briefs. She traced it with her fingers and was rewarded by his all-over body shiver. Her eyesight skidded back up his chest and saw the wicked-looking scar on his right shoulder. It appeared new and still just a bit angry. She started to touch it, but he stopped her by taking her hand in his and carrying it to his mouth. He nibbled on her fingers and she sighed just before her eyelids started to lower as if against her will.

"May I love you?" he whispered.

"Oh, yes," she replied.

His body reacted to the soft answer as if heavy chains had just loosed an anchor. Her underwear and his were torn away and he pulled her down on top of him as he knelt on the floor.

Although their foreplay had been short, it had been intense, and she was as rabid for him as he apparently was for her. He took long enough to dig a condom out of his pocket and put it on with brisk efficiency.

"Ah, I do so love a man who comes prepared," she said.

Her laugh at his smile quickly turned to a groan when put his hands under her buttocks and lifted her so her legs were spread wide and resting against his hipbones. She wrapped her arms around his neck and the result was that their bodies were perfectly aligned.

When he seated himself deep inside her wet pussy, Abby felt closer to him than she ever had to any other man. A rippling sigh escaped and she felt the give and take of her inner muscles as she adjusted to the wonderful size and heat of him.

It took only three thrusts until she found her release. His groan of satisfaction matched her cry as they plummeted over the edge of release together.

*   *   *

A long time later Oliver opened his eyes.

She was sitting on his lap and his knees were bent holding them up. He was still nestled in her warmth, even though he was only semi-hard now. He could see a light dusting of freckles across her face and was entranced by the way her eyelashes curled gently against the soft skin of her round cheek. Slowly, as his mind began to catch up with his body, he realized the floor underneath him, although covered in lush carpet, was still hard. However, he honestly didn't know if he had enough energy left to move.

As if she could read his mind, Abby sighed and stretched against his body. The friction of her soft skin against his was arousing and, though he would have thought seconds ago that there was no way he could go for round two, his body had other thoughts. But when she placed her hands on his chest and pushed, he allowed it, stretching out on his back on the floor. When she followed and stretched out on top of him, he thought that was dandy as well.

"God, you feel good," she purred, nibbling and licking her way across his chest. Then she worked her way down and across his rib cage as she moved and separated them. He had a moment's regret for that as his arms were suddenly empty. "And your taste, even right here. I think I could survive on it alone. I never knew a man of the water would taste like this. You're tart but not tangy, and salty but not briny."

Abby paused a few seconds to look up at him through her curtain of satiny hair. It fell in loose waves around her face and down to her shoulders. She looked like Circe luring sailors to take their chances against the rocks. She scooted even lower on his body and removed his spent condom. She touched his cock gently as if examining it were a sweet treat.

"You know, I did some research on the Coast Guard," Abby murmured.

Her words made a humming sound against the skin of his abdomen. His muscles quivered like he was doing a grueling round of crunches.

"I learned that your motto is *Semper Paratus*—Always Prepared."

If his brain had been anything more than mush at that moment, he might have found words to reply. All he could do was grab a fistful of her hair, whether to stop her or keep her in place forever, he couldn't tell.

"Are you truly always prepared, Petty Officer Robinson?"

Before he could do more than moan, her mouth swooped lower. She moved again and this time her head was at his groin and her hips were astride his chest. He could see her beautiful ass and, when she leaned forward and starting licking the underside of his cock, he could see her rosy, full vaginal lips. It was hard to concentrate as the wonderful sensations of her working his cock were quickly driving him insane, but he wanted to give her some pleasure as well. He began slowly, licking from front to back. As he worked, he reveled in the smell and taste of her. He nuzzled her bush and explored the depth beyond. She was very wet and her moans were matched only by his own moans as she pleasured him beyond belief.

When he finally reached her firm, round button of desire Abby raised her head and his cock fell free from her mouth. Although he was dying for his own release, he wanted to give her this first. With her back as tight as an archer's bow, he continued to suckle her clit and managed to insert first one finger, then two, into her pussy. Her muscles clenched and released and the shiver that began at the top of her neck resonated throughout her body as her climax poured through her and onto his tongue.

When her shivers finally stopped, she turned her head and looked back at him. "Wow, that was unbelievabe," she said. "Your turn."

She turned back and began again to lick and fondle his cock and balls. He was so close it didn't take much, but when she tongued her way across his slit and took about three-quarters of him deep into her mouth, he felt his balls surge close to his body and cried, "I'm coming," to give her fair warning.

Instead of pulling away as he expected, she continued to work him, increasing his pleasure and sense of intimacy to the point his vision blurred.

*   *   *

They were lying in her bed together much later when she spoke. He was interested in everything she had to say, but he didn't know how much longer he was going to be awake. It had been a long week and it had ended with a strenuous rescue. It had been his first time back in action since the accident. That, coupled with the intense action he'd enjoyed with Abby the last few hours, and he was whipped.

"I never dreamed having my own real life hero could be so stimulating," she said.

He stiffened. "I'm no hero."

Her eyes, which had been starting to close, indicating she was just as tired as he was, opened. "Sure you are. You've been trained for it and you're very good at it. From the scar on your shoulder, I'd say you recently risked everything for someone else. That's a hero."

"No. That's hype. I'm just working for a paycheck like any other guy. I don't want to be a hero. I'm not cut out for it."

Abby was silent for a few moments. "Nobody who is just working for a living jumps into freezing water to rescue people. Nobody jumps from a helicopter into a stormy sea just for a paycheck. You are a hero."

"No, believe me, I'm not a hero. Heroes don't get other people shot. Heroes don't let their crew down in the clutch." He got up out of bed and started looking for his clothes. The fact they were strewn all over her apartment was a minor irritation. When he picked up her slinky red top, he turned off the feeling of desire rising in him as he remembered how much fun he'd had removing it from her.

She smiled gently at him. "Oh, Oliver Robinson, you're a hero. Perhaps, at the moment, you're a wounded hero. But there's no doubt about it. Look how you rescued Billy. Look how you saved me. I thought I could save Billy, but the truth is I was already losing strength. If you hadn't been there, we'd have both drowned."

Oliver could feel the panic rising up from deep inside him. It built like a tidal wave starting in the pit of his stomach and rising until it was nearly choking the breath from him. He had to stop this. This minute.

"I'm not a hero. Heroes don't get busted from Lieutenant down to Petty Officer. Heroes don't get kicked out of the top rescue station in the Guard and sent to the wading pool." He dropped his clothes and strode over to where she stood. He gripped her arms and pulled her closer to him. "I'm a has-been, baby, so if you're looking for a little hero worship, you've got the wrong guy. I'm not your hero. I'm nobody's hero."

"Oliver, Oliver, please, you're hurting me," she said.

It was then he realized he had picked her up and was holding her by her arms. It was then he saw the fear in her eyes behind the tears streaming down her face. Now he'd done it. He'd reached a place he'd never thought he'd be. A place he'd been fearing he would fall into, but had hoped he'd have the control needed to keep anyone else from suffering from his anger. But like everything else since the moment ten miles south of Miami on a late February night, he'd screwed this up as well.

He set Abby back on the floor. The marks on her arms were already mocking him, letting him know just what a worthless brute he truly was.

"I'm sorry," he said. He turned, picked up his clothes and left.

*   *   *

Abby felt tears dripping out of her eyes and onto her cheeks. She'd been crying ever since Oliver had stormed out of her apartment. Not for herself, but for him. He was so hurt, so bruised that she wondered what she could ever do to help him heal. And healing was obviously what he needed. Not only from the physical wounds of whatever had happened to him, but emotional healing as well.

If he wouldn't let her in, what could she do? She smiled. *A lot.* She rose and went to shower.

She was a teacher and a teacher taught. She could teach him how to let her in.

CHAPTER 3

"Petty Officer Oliver Robinson reporting as ordered, sir." Oliver stood in front of his Group commander and waited for his response.

"Stand easy, Robinson." The commander paused for a few seconds and continued looking over the papers in front of him.

Oliver didn't have to have ESP to know the commander was reviewing his file.

"So, you've decided not to ship over, huh? Why?"

"Sir, I think I've done my turn. It's time to do something else."

"Hhhm, after ten years you're giving it up? This doesn't have anything to do with the incident in Miami, does it?"

Oliver swallowed back the bile of revulsion that rose in his throat. He'd been in turmoil ever since he'd walked out on Abby nearly a week ago. "Sir, I won't lie and say no. But Miami isn't the only factor involved."

The commander was silent for a few more moments. "Son—I hope you don't mind me calling you son. Even though you're not as young as most of my men, you're still a lot younger than me."

"Sir," Oliver acknowledged. He could insist on formality, but he didn't want to give the CO any grief. It was a small thing and he seemed to be a pretty good guy.

"You were completely cleared by the review board. The accident in Miami was not your fault." The commander held up his hand, warding off Oliver's instinctive reply. "I know that isn't always enough. I wasn't always a commander, you know."

"I didn't think you had always been, sir. I know how the Guard works," Oliver said.

"I know you do. I also know losing your crew and your boat, in addition to nearly bleeding to death while waiting to be rescued isn't something a man forgets. But, son, you need to put it behind you. You've had a good and stellar career in the Guard. What do you think you're going to find when you're no longer in it?"

Oliver started to come up with the standard response he'd given to everyone from the regional command to the shrinks on the hospital ship. But he looked in the amazingly kind, knowing eyes of his new commander and knew that answer wouldn't fly.

"I don't know what I expect, sir. I just know I can't go on being what the Guard wants," Oliver said. "The Guard needs heroes. I'm not that guy any more."

His commander sighed and all Oliver could hear for a few minutes was the sound of the large clock on the wall ticking.

"Okay. But you still owe the Coast Guard six more weeks. I won't allow you any easy duty. You'll pull boat detail and make inspections just like everyone else on this crew. Is that clear?"

Oliver straightened to attention. Personal time was over. "Aye, aye, sir."

"Part of our mission here is education. With that in mind, I want you to go over and talk to a group of people from one of the schools who were on the tour boat last week."

"Me, sir? Wouldn't one of the married guys be better? How about Danheiser? I think he's got a couple of kids." Oliver felt panic rise.

He didn't want to be talking to civilians. What if one of them were Abby? He felt his muscles tense at the thought of seeing her. He'd managed to keep from going over to her apartment on the rest of his weekend off, even though it had taken every bit of his resolve. He'd actually breathed easier when his three days were over and he'd headed back to the duty station.

"Nope. You're the one. Besides, Danheiser's fresh out of the academy. He doesn't have any field experience, except the short time he's been here. I want someone who can talk to these folks, not only about boating safety, but about the Coast Guard and what we do. By the way, I also want you to present a certificate to that young teacher who jumped into the water after the boy. That took a lot of guts, don't you think?"

"Yes, sir," Oliver replied. "As it so happens, she lives in the same apartment building as I do. I only met her after the rescue, though."

The commander looked at Oliver for a moment, then laughed. "Damn, Robinson. I know you had a reputation as a lady's man in Miami, but this is quick, even for you."

Oliver shook his head. "It isn't like…" *What?* He couldn't very well tell his commander he'd had the most amazing sex of his life, then had pretty much fucked and run, could he?

"Whatever," the commander said. "I may be old, but I'm not dead. The ladies do love the uniform, don't they? I met my wife my first week at the station nearly twenty years ago, so I do remember.

"At any rate, during the ceremony this afternoon, give the lady a certificate. Not many people would've done that. From what the doctors said, she probably kept the kid from going into respiratory arrest. They're expecting you this afternoon at three."

Before Oliver could protest more, the commander ended the meeting with a simple, "Dismissed."

Oliver saluted, turned and left. This was one thing he wouldn't miss when he got out of the Guard. No more going where he was told without any say in the matter. Why him? *Didn't anyone understand he wasn't the one to be talking about the Guard?* Couldn't anyone just let him do his job and stay below the radar? *Damn it!*

As he was leaving the commandant's office, it dawned on him. The problem wasn't with Abby or anyone else, it was with him. Instead of going to his quarters to catch some Zs, Oliver turned and walked outside the Buffalo headquarters. Group Buffalo was situated at the head of the Niagara River and the eastern end of Lake Erie. As Oliver walked to the point that separated the river from the lake, he thought about all he'd been through the last few months. He stuck his hands in his pockets and watched as colorful sailboats made their way either into the river and Erie Canal, or turned to ride the wind on the open lake.

As a warm breeze ruffled his shirt and the sun bounced so brightly off the waves that it was nearly blinding, Oliver went back in his mind to the night in Miami. As he replayed the events, he tried his best to figure a way to have kept things from spinning out of control. In a way that hadn't been possible before, he examined every action and reaction of, not only himself, but each member of his crew. Each time, each scenario led him to the same conclusion. He had been right, but so had the commander, so had Abby. He had done his job. He had performed his duty. In short, it hadn't been his fault, just as it hadn't been preventable.

As Oliver felt a sense of peace wash over him, he knew he only had one mission left to accomplish before moving forward with his life.

Unfortunately, that mission would have to wait a few hours until he met with Abby at school.

*   *   *

Where was she?

Oliver had been introduced to the principal of the Buffalo School, along with several of the senior staff members. She wasn't among them.

He'd also been introduced to several parents, among them a very effusive and grateful Mrs. and Mr. Borrelli. It was through the Borrellis he learned about Abby's troubles with some of the other parents and the school board.

It angered him when he learned some people were using the accident as a reason to run her out of her job. He thought back to the selfless courage she'd shown by going in after Billy. There were a lot of men and women who'd failed to make the grade at the Coast Guard Academy who hadn't shown half the courage of Abby had. Granted diving in to save a child was reckless, but it'd also been heroic. Anything could have happened with Billy. Oliver said as much to the Borrellis and it seemed they agreed wholeheartedly with him.

He told them he didn't know what kind of teacher she was, but he knew if he had a child, Oliver would want Abby in his or her corner. The Borrellis agreed and assured him she was just as caring and dedicated to her teaching duties.

But Oliver wanted to tell Abby that in person. Now he cursed every moment of his wasted free time when he could have been spending it with her, when he could have convinced her she was the hero, and not him.

Instead, Oliver was stuck giving a talk to people he didn't want to know and spending the afternoon without her in his arms.

He smiled at all the people in the small conference room waiting to hear him speak, while his mind was repeating one thing over and over. When he was off, he'd do everything to find Abby and make her his.

But first there was something he could do.

*   *   *

Abby looked at her watch and swore. She was going to be late and she didn't want to be late. *Not this afternoon!*

She pulled into the lot of the elementary school and put her car in park. She was nervous. She shouldn't be. The big meeting, the one that had held her career in the balance, had been over for an hour. She would be keeping her job—at least as long as budget cuts didn't force the district into layoffs.

That wasn't what made her nervous. What made her nervous was seeing Oliver again. She'd left him alone for the remainder of his weekend, even though she'd known he was in his apartment. She figured he needed time. She knew she did. And Abby had used the extra time to plot her strategy.

First, she'd done some research on the Coast Guard, then she'd called up her best friend from college. Betsy was married to a Coast Guard pilot and they were stationed in North Carolina. The conversation had been informative in more ways than one. Betsy had told Abby the general gist of what had happened to Oliver in Miami. Betsy's information had re-confirmed what Abby had sensed from the beginning. Oliver was a hero all right, but he was one whose soul was in desperate need of anchoring. He was allowing guilt and self-doubt to cloud his entire life.

Well, Abby wouldn't stand for it. She was going to make Oliver understand that he'd done everything he could possibly do and more. Abby had never consciously tried to "get" a man before. Then again, she'd never met a man like Oliver before. So, today was the first day of Abby's campaign to restore Oliver's soul. She would not fail.

*   *   *

Oliver knew the second she slipped in the door at the rear of the room. He was talking about daily operations of a Coast Guard unit, but he could almost feel the air in the room heat up by ten degrees. It was a wonder all the other men didn't feel it as well.

He paused and then continued. "So, in addition to education and inspection of boaters and boats, we also handle search and rescue. As most of you know, we used the search and rescue techniques last week with the *Niagara Belle.*"

The Borrellis were smiling at him. Oliver passed over them and looked straight at Abby. "In truth, though, the rescue was accomplished by one of your teachers, Ms. Smithton. She realized Billy Borrelli was overboard before any of the rescuers did and jumped in to save him. That, folks, is what heroism is about.

"We in the Coast Guard have a creed that every man and woman, enlisted or officer, follows. One line of it says, "I shall sell life dearly to an enemy of my country, but give it freely to rescue those in peril." Your Ms. Smithton did that and should be applauded for it. I applaud her for it and have a certificate from our commanding officer to present to her in recognition of that brave act."

He paused and waited for the applause, which was started by the Borrellis, but soon encompassed everyone in the room.

"Ms. Smithton, if you'd please come here."

She walked forward and he noticed the pleasure on her face. He hoped it was only the beginning of what he'd see there before the afternoon was through.

"Ms. Smithton, this certificate says: For heroism and dedication to saving and preserving life, we sincerely thank you and give you the Coast Guard Certificate of Merit."

Everyone in the room rose to their feet and applauded. When Abby reached for the certificate, he held his end keeping her close to him. "I applaud you as well and wonder if your courage will extend to offering an idiot a second chance?"

Abby looked at him. "I might, but I may need a bit more convincing," she said softly.

He smiled. "Convincing I'm very good at. How about at my place at nineteen-hundred hours tomorrow?"

Abby smiled and saluted. "Aye, aye, sir."

His smile dimmed a little. "There are some things I have to tell you." He paused. "About what happened in Miami with my crew."

Abby nodded. "I know. I'll be willing to listen, but you don't have to tell me until you're ready."

"It may make you feel differently—"

"No." She placed her fingers over his own and squeezed lightly.

He could see she was highly aware of him. Could she feel the tingle running across his nerves and deep in his core. He looked deeply in her eyes for another few seconds, then smiled again. "Okay. Well then, tomorrow, nineteen-hundred."

"Tomorrow," Abby promised.

*   *   *

Abby nervously opened the door to her apartment to go to Oliver's. It was eighteen-forty and she was early, but she couldn't wait any longer. She giggled. She was already thinking in military time, like she was the one in the Coast Guard. She was wearing the outfit she'd been wearing on their date, without the jacket. She was hoping it would have the same effect on him tonight as it did the first night. She also had a little surprise she hoped he'd like.

When she opened the door, he was standing there. He was blindingly handsome in khakis and a buttoned-down oxford shirt. But his startling blue eyes shining with what she hoped was love, along with lust, made her catch her breath.

"Hi," he said.

"Hi, yourself," she managed. "I was just coming over…I hope I'm not late."

"No. I'm early, but I couldn't wait another minute," he said. He took her hand and carried it to his lips. He placed a soft kiss on her palm and she felt a large chunk of her heart start to melt. "This is for you. Hope you like it."

It was then she noticed the perfect, peach-colored, long-stemmed rose he was holding in his other hand. Before she could take it, he moved it in a caress across her forehead, down her cheeks and over her lips. The stroke was tender and arousing. Abby knew that, if he kept this up, she was going to be a puddle at his feet before they even got inside his apartment.

When he leaned towards her and let his lips follow the track of the rose, she was a goner. Her breath caught, and by the time his lips met hers in a kiss that was deep, soulful and full of promises, she had her arms wrapped around his neck and her body so close against his she could feel their heartbeats in perfect time.

The dull sound of the building door opening separated them a bit and he smiled gently.

"Come with me," he said, taking one hand and tucking it in the crook of his elbow. "I've got everything ready."

"I hope you didn't go to a lot of trouble. We could've just ordered in pizza or something."

"No trouble." He led her through the open door of his apartment, closing it after them.

It was pretty much what she expected—basic furnished apartment fare, except he had candles burning on all the tables in the living room and a small table set with a white linen cloth with a bottle of champagne nestled in a bucket of ice sitting to one side. She could see plates with warmer tops on them and elegant-looking silver at each setting.

He escorted her to one of the chairs and held it for her to sit.

"I see you're wearing my dress," he said.

She felt the caress of his fingers over her bare shoulder and managed to control the shiver that ran through her.

"Yes. I wanted to look special for you." She looked over her shoulder and up into his eyes. He was going to kiss her and she wanted it with every fiber in her being. He moved closer, then stopped and moved back bare inches. Abby released a sigh. He was going to take things slowly. Okay, she could do slow. She hoped.

He sat in the remaining chair. He leaned over and took the top off the first plate. On it sat a bed of shrimp and cocktail sauce. He took one and dipped it in thick sauce, then held it out to her. When she started to reach for it, he shook his head.

"Let me feed you," he whispered.

She leaned forward and he held the shrimp above her mouth. As she bit into it, she looked into his eyes. In them she saw promises she didn't dare to believe. After she took one bite, he pulled the shrimp away a bit and Abby felt some of the sauce drip onto her bottom lip. She started to lick it away, but he beat her to it, his lips and tongue doing a sensual dance against hers.

It was astonishing just how sensual it was to be fed this way, with each bite leading to shared hunger and even greater desire. By the time he had reached the last piece of shrimp, Abby was panting with desire and she didn't even take the bite he offered, going straight for his lips instead.

When they finished the appetizer, she looked at him, aroused and impatient.

"Abby, my love," he said. "I want to tell you about Miami."

"Oliver, my love," she repeated, "I want to hear about Miami as well, but first, will you let me love you?"

He smiled and she knew he was remembering when he'd asked her that question.

"Yes," he said coming back for another kiss.

Then he allowed her to stand, but only for a moment before he swung her into his arms.

"Wait a minute, this is my show," she said on a husky laugh.

"Oh, I plan to let you do all the work," he replied. "I just wanted to get us a little more comfortable."

Abby nodded. "Comfort is good."

He carried her through an apartment that mirrored her own and straight to a neat, if utilitarian, bedroom. The fact he had only just moved in was apparent with the lack of photos and mementos. But when he laid her on the bed and then began to undress, she forgot all about decorations.

"Wait," she ordered. "That's my job."

She got on her knees on the mattress and moved to the edge, where she could reach him. He'd undone the top button of his shirt and that's where she began. With each button she undid, she tasted him with her lips and tongue. Soon, his gleaming chest was covered with red lipstick outlines.

Keeping her touches light, she traced the outline of his nipples, pleased with the way Oliver shivered in response and how the hard buds tasted slightly salty with his desire when she suckled on them. When she removed the shirt completely, baring his chest to her eyes, she frowned at the sight of his scar. She moved closer and placed a gentle kiss on its center. Although he stiffened initially at the touch, he quickly relaxed.

"You sure you don't want to hear about Miami now?" he asked.

Abby could hear the desire in his gruff tone. She couldn't explain now with words, but maybe he would understand her actions.

"Later. We'll have all the time in the world later," she said.

But Abby's plan wasn't just to kiss the top half of him, as important as that was. Not wanting to be sidetracked, she moved lower. She removed his belt one loop at a time, then unsnapped and unzipped his pants. She got lost for a moment or two exploring the contours of his belly button and the way the line of hair from his chest arrowed down his washboard abs.

But soon she was back on track and kissing her way down to where his erection rose against the fabric of his briefs. She traced the outline his hard-on made with her tongue and he groaned and put his hands on her head. She thought for a moment he wanted to hold her in place, but he gently pulled her face back from his cock.

"I want to be inside you tonight when I come," he murmured.

Abby smiled up at him. "Sounds like just what I had in mind."

She laced the fingers of her right hand with his left and pulled him down on the bed. He stretched flat on his back and she helped him finish removing his underwear. When Oliver was naked, his cock rising proudly towards his abdomen, she moved off the bed to stand beside it. She could feel the hot lick of desire from his gaze as it passed over her and she shivered.

Slowly she lowered first one strap of her dress, then the second. She could feel the way her breasts were swelling and knew he could see the outline of her nipples in the fabric draped over her. Keeping her movements slow, when what Abby really wanted was to tear her clothes off and be as naked as him, was one of the hardest things she'd ever done.

Anticipation is sweet she believed, so she stripped for him, making each moment last as long as she could. By the time she was down to her black g-string bikini panties, she was panting like she'd just run a marathon, even though she'd hardly moved. She had a bit of satisfaction when she saw the rapid rise and fall of his chest indicating he was just as breathless as she.

"Surprise," she said. "Do you like them?"

"Hell, yeah," Oliver said. His hand reached for her and a finger stroked down the line of the panties, lingering on the edge that barely covered her thatch. She was already wet and wondered if he would be able to get his fingers inside her pussy from this position.

"Come closer, darlin'," he murmured.

Abby moved to obey and climbed on bed on top of him, her bent legs around his knees. She was sitting on his thighs and, for a moment, wondered if that would be uncomfortable for him, but the look in his eyes told her otherwise. He used both hands now, his left caressing her breasts, circling first one nipple, then the other. With his right hand, he continued tracing the outline of her pussy.

Her body was reacting with pleasure. Both her nipples were almost painfully hard and she could feel her cream easing its way past her enlarged lips and dampening the cloth of her panties.

Finally he slipped one finger inside her lips, and she cried out at the delight coursing through her. When he added a second large finger, she came like she was a rocket being fired through the air.

She was hardly down from that first high when he removed his fingers and pulled her higher on his body. He shucked the panties off her hips and pulled them down as far as her knees, then lifted her up a bit and fit her down over his cock. The feeling of his large, pulsing organ inside a tunnel still shivering from her first orgasm was almost overwhelming to her. But her muscles quickly adjusted, knowing another round of delight was waiting on the horizon.

She braced her hands on his chest and began to ride him slowly, up and down, then switching the motion so she was rotating her hips. His hips begin to dance as well, first countering and then completing each motion she made.

"You feel so damn good," he gasped. "I love everything about you. I will never have enough of you."

She gasped at his words and felt as one with Oliver. She let her hands slide further up his chest until her hips were tilted forward and her face was level with his. The position tilted them so the angle of his cock and her pelvis gave them the deepest penetration. It also meant that every forward thrust and retreat sent pulses of pleasure arrowing into her sweetest spot of pleasure.

It was as if they were in a warm, glowing bubble where time stood still, where the world stopped, where they were concerned only with the pleasure each was feeling and sending it back to the other doubled and tripled in intensity.

She felt his release at the same moment as hers crested.

"I love you," she cried as she felt his seed rush from him.

"You are so beautiful, you know?"

She didn't know how long it took her to reach the point of speech, but she knew, when she was finally able to mutter the words, they were still entwined. Her head was against his neck and her lips were able to nibble on his strong breastbone without any effort. She could feel their come leaking out of her pussy, but didn't feel any embarrassment, just complete fulfillment.

He grunted. "Just what a guy wants to hear."

"It should be. Not just beautiful on the outside, but here as well." Now Abby's hand and mouth moved back up his chest and hovered over where his heart beat. "You know, when I said you're a hero, that's what I was talking about. You have this amazing heart, this amazing capacity to care."

He placed a finger under her chin and raised her face so she was looking into his eyes rather than at his chest. "You should know. Your heart is much stronger than mine."

Abby shook her head. "No. I jumped in after one boy. You jump in after hundreds. Day after day."

Oliver frowned. "I can't save them all." He released a long, shuddering breath. "I haven't saved them all. Not even close. In Miami I started believing my own hype."

She was silent for a moment, waiting for him to finish.

"Just before the last operation in Miami, my crew and I had rescued this family during a hurricane. I don't know why, but we became media darlings. Other crews out of our station rescued people, but there was something about this one family that made everyone call us heroes. It was heady, a rush.

"So when the chance came to take down a drug dealer bringing in a large shipment of cocaine, I...we took risks we shouldn't have. The result was I got shot and my crew was lost. I took a demotion from Lieutenant to Petty Officer after the whole thing."

He paused as if he expected her to say something derogatory. She wouldn't oblige him.

"Did the Coast Guard want to strip you of your rank?" she asked, keeping her anger at the system under wraps.

"No, no. They wanted to give me a medal because I got the drug dealer. He lived and is in prison. But I lost the rest of my crew."

She nodded and kissed his neck gently. "Oh, I see."

His hand, which had been rubbing up and down her spine, stopped.

"No, I don't think you do see. I lost four good men and women. They were the heroes, not me. I saved a crook and sacrificed friends. That isn't heroic, that's idiotic."

Abby could tell he was still wrapped in his grief from the incident. And no wonder. But perhaps what he needed wasn't more sympathy, but a good old-fashioned kick in the butt.

"Oh, I see. So you equate heroism with Godliness."

He paused. She could tell he was a bit taken aback by her words.

"No. But don't you think being a hero has responsibility? Don't you think a hero should save everyone?"

Abby hummed as she wrapped her arms around his neck and hugged him tightly against her. "Of course not. No one could. You're human. You did the best you could in the situation and you've bled for every friend you've lost. You've mourned for each of them. That's what makes you a true hero."

He hugged her back and kissed her as well. "You make me almost believe it."

"Good. Maybe if I keep saying it for the next hundred years, you'll truly believe it."

He smiled. "That sounds about right. Because I'm not going to let you go for at least the next hundred years."

"Aye, aye, sir."

PARTY FOR TWO

———————————

CHAPTER 1

Ben walked up to the door of the quaint, unassuming Cape Cod style house wondering what in the world he was doing.

The last thing he wanted was to spend hours with a bunch of people he hadn't seen in twenty years, reminiscing over times that hadn't been that good.

He looked again at the plain but appealing invitation that had been stuck in his mail box. *Ellen Snyder.* Just seeing the way her signature sprawled across the bottom of the paper in easy, bold curves made his fingers itch and the blood rush to his cock with reassuring haste.

Jeezus. He was coming up hard on fifty. He'd raised two wonderful children, had lost his wife of twenty years to breast cancer and was finally getting to live his life the way he wanted. So why did just seeing a name from his childhood cause him to react like a adolescent having his first wet dream?

Ben couldn't answer that question. He did know that was the biggest reason he was willing to go to her house for this party tonight. If there was any chance he could see her, talk to her—alone—for five minutes, he figured it would be worth it.

He was ten minutes early. Except for one time, twenty years ago, he was routinely early. It had a lot to do with his time spent in the Marines. You couldn't change overnight. Even if he was letting his hair grow longer than it had been since 1970, underneath the streaked salt-and-pepper strands was a brush cut just waiting to come out.

Some of his ex-recruits from Parris Island would probably laugh their asses off if they could see him now or heard about his new career. At this point he didn't give a good damn. He was finally going to do something he wanted. He was going to write sexy thrillers and had an agent asking to see his first manuscript. He knew it was a long-shot that the agent would want to represent him and an even longer shot that his book would ever be published.

But he was determined to take this shot. It was part of the reason he was back in Tonawanda. It was the place of his birth and the house he'd just moved back into late last week was his family home. His parents had died six weeks ago in their sleep. Ben figured that's the way they would have wanted it.

His children thought he'd gone a little bonkers coming back to this sleepy town at the point where the Erie Canal and Niagara River joined. His kids, busy building their own lives in South Carolina, thought he was going through some kind of mid-life crisis. Or, as his son had said last night on the phone, maybe he was in some deep depression.

Ben was doing neither. He couldn't get either of his kids to believe that. Well, they were living their lives and they'd just have to adjust to the fact their father was going to live his too.

Which brought him back to the present, standing at the bottom step of Ellen's porch. He could see low lights on in the front room, but he couldn't see much else. He smiled as he remembered the time when they'd been five and he'd made her scream, partly in fear, partly in humor, when he tried putting a frog down her shirt. He could still hear her girlish laughter ringing in his ears as she'd proclaimed how the frog had tickled. He'd stolen his first kiss that night as the sun was setting over the river and the sounds of the night were falling around them. No matter where he'd gone, what he'd done, he'd never forgotten it.

Ben took a deep breath. Maybe he'd get lucky and it would be a while before the rest of her guests arrived. He would use the time to get re-acquainted with his first love.

*   *   *

"God, what's taking him so long?" Ellen whispered as she stood on the other side of the door. She knew he was on her front walk. She'd been watching him from behind the blinds. Frankly, she'd been worried he wouldn't show, so, when she'd seen him cross the grass separating their houses, she'd done the happy dance in jubilation. This was a calculated gamble. One so great she was sure she was about to lose everything. But that had been five minutes ago.

Had she jinxed it? Had her happy dance been in vain?

No, no. She couldn't let negative thoughts win the day. She wasn't the nervous young girl who'd loved Ben Tolley from the day she first saw him. She wasn't the woman who wore such rose-colored glasses that she'd turned a pumpkin into a prince because she was trying to find a replacement for Ben. She wasn't the wallflower who stayed in that bad marriage for ten years, even though her slug of a husband was busy diddling everything that moved inside Tonawanda and out.

No, Ellen was her own woman now. She ran an eclectic shop that catered to big beautiful women and their needs—intimate and not. Her shop BBW, which stocked everything from large-sized lingerie to sexy toys for the discriminating woman, was fast becoming the talk of all of Western New York.

And Ellen was finally, as she came ever closer to her fiftieth birthday, completely comfortable in her own skin. She wasn't ever going to be a size five and she was happy about it. Not only that, but she found she was more popular with men than ever before. So why was she sweating like the girl she'd been nearly forty-five years ago when she'd touched her lips to Ben's for the first time?

Ellen closed her eyes, then ran a shaky hand down the wonderful silk of her almost see-through black lace gown. She wasn't going to wait any longer. The man of her dreams was here. It was time to welcome him to her party.

Her hand was on the door knob to open it when his knock rattled the wood.

"Oh!" The sound scared her so she jumped back a step and promptly stubbed her heel on an uneven piece of flooring. "Shit, shit, shit, that hurts," she cursed a bit. Not the best way to start the evening. She shook off the thought, took a deep breath and opened the door.

"Hello, Ben. Come on in."

CHAPTER 2

Ben felt as if every ounce of breath in his lungs had been sucked out, like he'd fallen off the top of the Victory Tower without a harness and landed on his back. In front of him was the most stunning woman he'd ever seen. She had long, flowing red hair, with one streak of white from the top to the bottom on the right side. Her hazel green eyes, which had haunted him over the years, were bright with welcome and he felt like he was sinking into their warmth. He pulled his gaze away from her eyes and then got hung up on her mouth. Her lips were wide and full, wet, red and ripe. He had a sudden vivid picture of those lips wrapped around his rock hard cock, servicing it like the most schooled courtesan. He shook his head slightly. He had to do something because every ounce of blood was hurtling southward like a laser-guided missile. So he took in the rest of her.

Mistake. Big mistake.

She was wearing this black, filmy lace gown that left the creamy, white skin of her shoulders bare. There was a smattering of freckles over her chest and one—he blinked not really believing what he was seeing—deep red beauty mark nestled right at the top of her bountiful cleavage.

Game, set and match. He'd was aced before he'd even entered her house. It took every once of his control not to fasten his lips on that mark and live there for the next eon or two.

*   *   *

"Ben, I'm so glad you could come to my party. It's so good to see you again. Come in."

Her voice sounded low and husky. Ellen almost giggled with glee. The look on his face was priceless. His eyes were lit with wonderful male appreciation and, from the way the front of his pants were starting to get pretty full, she'd hit a home run on her first swing. If the rest of the night was as successful, all the worry and second guesses were going to be worth it.

She reached for his hand and drew him inside her house. While he was appreciating the view, she took stock herself. He was just as gorgeous as she remembered. His hair was full and the way the gray mixed in with his black strands gave new meaning to aging gracefully. She'd expected, since he just recently retired from the Corps, he'd be in good shape and she wasn't wrong. He wasn't thin, but simply solid.

From the breadth of his shoulders, down over his well-defined pecs, which even the modest cotton golf-type shirt couldn't disguise, down to his washboard flat stomach, he was the stuff her fantasies had been dreaming up for the last twenty years. For a second, Ellen wished she was that size five. Then her gaze arrowed back below his belt.

She may not be an expert on alpha males, but she did know they didn't have that kind of reaction to someone they found unattractive.

She smiled and hoped he wouldn't start thinking he was the fly and she the spider.

"Can I get you something cold, or"—she paused just for a second—"hot."

His Adam's apple bobbed quickly. If she hadn't been watching him so closely, Ellen would have missed it.

"Cold, I think. I'm a little early," he said. "I hope I didn't come before you're ready."

Damn, Ellen thought. The way he said "come" had her ready to cream her panties. That is, if she'd been wearing any.

"Oh, no, you've got perfect timing," she assured him, leading him from the hall to the living room.

She had everything set up and as she looked it over, she wondered if she was still setting herself up for a tremendous fall. The lights were turned low and there was a fire burning in the fireplace. It, considering she was using a special vanilla-scented log that a sales rep had tried to get her to stock in her store, might be a little over the top considering it was late August, but she'd wanted to pull out everything in her arsenal. So, along with the fire, she had blues playing low in the background and the shades drawn against the early evening sun.

A small round table, just for two, was placed to the left of the fireplace. She'd moved her traditional wooden dining room table into the kitchen that afternoon. Beside the table was a bottle of champagne, open to breathe and chilling in a bucket of ice. There were two place settings and two, tall, white candlesticks placed between the settings. Ellen hoped Ben would see it and not run right out of her house when he realized this party was just for two.

"I hope you don't mind. I wanted us to have the chance to catch up a bit," she said, fisting one of her hands at her side, preparing for the heartbreak if she'd over-played her option and he either left right now, or worse, laughed at her.

Instead he turned those soul-stirring blue eyes on her and smiled slowly. Ellen felt her insides melting even more. She'd been dreaming of this moment for so long and now it appeared to be going better than she hoped.

"I think it's perfect."

He moved then and pulled out one of the chairs for her. Ellen stood for a moment wanting to capture the picture in her memory forever. He stood smiling at her, the low lights and the glow from the fire keeping his face dark, but providing a small halo around his head. The candles were flickering a bit and the white table cloth and red dinnerware were the perfect touch. She had set this scene up to seduce. Instead, with one simple movement, he'd turned the tables on her, becoming the seducer instead.

She smiled. Well, the night was young. Perhaps they would switch roles many times before the night was done.

"Dinner or..."—she paused, looking over her shoulder at him hoping he could read her meaning in her eyes—"first?"

"Or," he whispered as he pulled her into his arms. "Definitely 'or' now *and* later."

His breath caressed the skin of her cheek seconds before she felt the soft touch of his lips there. Then he moved lower joining them in their first taste of passion.

His lips were full, warm and tasted of mint. Ellen didn't know why, but suddenly she was starved for mint. This wasn't a cold mint like found in ice cream, but was infused with a heat that moved through her blood like a drug. She felt his tongue as it licked deliciously at her bottom lip. She was ready and willing to open for him, but he seemed to be in no hurry, willing to just enjoy the sensation of their liplock for as long as she wanted. She'd longed for a man with slow hands, one who knew how to love a woman. She hadn't believed it possible to find one with patient lips.

Ben filled the bill in more ways than one. So Ellen relaxed against him fully, letting him set the pace and the tone for the night.

It seemed to be the signal he was waiting for because he pulled her closer to him, widening his legs a bit and started a slow, sensual dance without moving an inch.

His hands were everywhere and nowhere. It was maddening. It was delightful.

A brush of his fingers over an eyebrow and then down her nose before lingering on her full bottom lip, tugging it down as if opening her wide for him.

She was ready, more than. Before she could take his digit inside, it was gone.

Down her neck and resting at the spot where her pulse was already pounding like a runaway train.

His fingers moved again, this time skirting down the slope of her breast before circling once, twice, three times over her burgeoning nipple, bringing her excitement up a notch, but leaving her far from satisfied.

Had she wanted slow? She must have been crazy. Ellen realized with a start that he was leaning against the back of her couch, his hips resting on the top edge. Ben was a tall man, which was nice because she wasn't a little woman.

At five-nine-and-a-half in stocking feet, she still towered over a lot of the available men, which is why she always wore low-heeled shoes.

Her height wasn't a disadvantage with Ben. He was six-three at least, and when he leaned backward and pulled her closer to him, she fit perfectly.

She ran her hands up his chest and wound her arms around his neck. She sighed again and felt him respond. She wanted to let her weight rest fully against him, but she also didn't want to send him falling backward over the couch. She had big plans for him tonight and they didn't include a trip to the emergency room for back problems.

As if he could read her mind, he bit her bottom lip, then sucked it into his mouth. The shock raced through her like she was a sports car on a racetrack, and her pussy muscles clenched wildly in response.

His hands, which had been clutching at her waist, moved downward. She felt a breeze on her legs as his fingers slowly walked the edge of her gown above her knees and over her thighs. Finally those strong, pleasantly rough hands were cupping her butt and pulling her even closer into the niche of his hips.

Ellen felt a moment's regret. She'd given up on the glut exercises a few months ago when she realized her butt was never going to resemble that of the eighteen-year-old instructor who taught the aerobics class at her club. She had been at peace with the decision. Now she wondered if she'd given up a little too soon.

He moved his lips away from hers a fraction. "I'm feeling a little hesitation here?" he murmured.

Ellen smiled and hoped he couldn't read the regret in her eyes.

"No hesitation on my part," she answered. "I was just giving you a chance to go while the going was good."

His hand moved slowly on her cheek, long, strong fingers flexing, then releasing. She felt the touch like an arrow of desire cutting through her. Her outer lips were swelling and she could feel a build-up of fluid behind her walls.

"I'm not looking to go anywhere," he said. "In fact, I'm ready to get this party moving."

Still holding her locked against him, he moved with the agility of a much younger man, sliding over the back of the sofa. Before she could do more than blink, she was looking up at him, the sofa cushions at her back and his wonderfully strong body touching her in all the parts that mattered and some that never had before.

"Oh, my," she said.

His smile was brilliant, his perfect teeth a white slash against the tanned contours of his face.

"Yeah, this dog has a few tricks left in the bunker," he said.

Ellen felt a laugh gurgling. He caught the sound with his mouth as he kissed her with a slow thoroughness that had her spinning beyond desire into raging need. Ellen had read about toe-curling kisses in the erotic novels she inhaled like Godiva chocolate. She hadn't believed they existed outside of fiction. She now knew they did.

When he finally let her take a break to breathe, she couldn't help the sigh that came from her mouth.

"Wow," she said. "Do all Marines kiss like that?"

"I don't know, since I don't go around kissing Marines," he answered. "But if you don't mind, I'll get back to the business at hand."

Ellen couldn't even nod as he was kissing her again. This one was even better than the last. She could feel just how aroused he was as he lay with his jean-clad hips in perfect alignment with her own. His erection was strong and sure as it pressed against her belly.

Despite his desire, Ellen knew Ben wasn't in any hurry to finish this off. It seemed he was satisfied just kissing her. Of course, if this was the way he kissed everyone, she could certainly vouch that the patience and practice hadn't been wasted.

Ellen wasn't a virgin, not by more years than she cared to think about. She had been kissed before—by a lot of toads and a few princes. She knew now, though, she'd never been kissed like this. Her breathing hitched and caught, then stuttered back into action like she was running a marathon.

Incredibly, she was getting turned on. Not a mild arousal normal from a sweet kiss, but a deep, soul-burning, womb-swelling desire. The heat began where their lips touched and rode through her bloodstream, across her limbs, sending every nerve ending in her body into full alert. And when his hands picked up where they'd left off before, moving back to her breasts and plucking at her nipples instead of just circling them, while he was giving her this bone-melting kiss, Ellen felt as if her body had been sent into high gear.

When her orgasm swelled over her like the tide of a flood, she moaned deep into his mouth, wanting nothing but the taste of him on her lips and tongue and the feel of him pleasuring her breasts. Breathing wasn't important. It was, in fact, downright expendable.

But every breath she took was him, his taste, his smell, his being drumming into her soul. His hands were instruments of delight, coursing down her body, flexing into her butt and holding her flush against him. But his lips were a weapon of unforgettable passion. When she crested a second time on the wave of desire, Ellen knew kissing would never be the same.

He finally left her lips and moved lower to nibble his way down her neck. She was heaving, drawing great gasps of air into her lungs, feeling as if every nerve ending in her body was still exposed, raw and needy. He palmed first one breast then the other and she knew he was pleased at the fullness of them by the way he was murmuring.

"God, you are so beautiful," he whispered, then lowered his mouth so she felt the wetness of his lips and tongue on her nipple through the fabric of her gown. She could feel her insides clamoring and gearing up for another orgasm.

How was it possible? She had come twice, but her body was as hungry as if she hadn't come at all. And he hadn't even gotten to her sweet spot yet.

"God, Ben." The words seemed to take all her energy between her gasps. "Please, I need more."

He raised his face and she saw the glitter of raw desire in his eyes. She could feel the hard, strong outline of his cock through his pants and her silk. She also could feel a dampness as well, telling her he hadn't been under control the whole time either. For a moment, she felt bereft. She wanted, needed, his essence in her, not wasted in cloth.

Gathering strength she didn't know she had left in her boneless body, she pushed him away from her. In a move that would've made one of the gym bimbettes proud, she reversed their positions. As he sprawled on his back, she moved so she was kneeling on the floor, looking up at him.

Keeping her eyes on his face, she opened his pants and lightly traced the shape of him in his white skivvies. They were stretched taut and his cock was so extended she could see the tip of it edging past the waistband of his shorts. She ran her finger across the elastic, stopping just short of his weeping tip. She bit her lip. Not touching him, really touching him, was incredibly hard.

But she wanted to show him that he wasn't the only one who understood patience and delayed gratification.

When his entire body tightened, she smiled in triumph. Rising on her knees, she let her tongue trace the area her finger had marked.

Once, twice, three times. Coming so close, but not hitting the spot. On the fourth pass, she veered down his briefs, letting her tongue trace the length of him through the white cotton.

She could feel his heat, smell his musk. The cotton was stretched tight now.

"Ellen, please," he begged.

"Oh, I intend to," she murmured and, giving them both what they were aching for, she slid her hands under the edge of his shorts and pulled them down, releasing his gorgeous cock to her sight for the first time.

It was thick and wide, just long enough she knew she'd feel filled. The head was wet with evidence of his first orgasm. It beckoned Ellen like a large cone of ice cream. But she knew it would heat her insides like a roaring fire.

Before she could think about him filling up her needy pussy, she had to have a taste.

Wanting only to draw out their pleasure as long as he had with his lovemaking to her mouth, she took him slowly into her mouth.

She licked her way around the tip of him, over the bulbous head, tasting the edge of the crown before moving slowly from the outside to the middle. She wanted to delve her tongue deep into his slit, but decided to hold off on that pleasure until later. Instead, she moved back to the edge and worked her way down his shaft, moving down one side, then up the other.

All the time her lips and tongue were busy learning the shape and taste of him, her hands were also learning the feel of him. She cupped his large testicles, then traced down the line of flesh that separated them. She felt them swell in her hands and cupped first one, then the other and started a gentle massage.

All the while her mouth was working him. Up one side and down the other, over and over. His musk was growing stronger, signaling how his arousal was growing. Funny thing was her arousal was increasing, too, with each downward stroke of her tongue.

When she thought neither could stand the teasing any longer, she took him fully into her mouth.

He held her head against him and moaned.

"God, Ellen, you're killing me," he said.

She laughed and the vibration must have been even more of a turn-on for him. He groaned again and began thrusting his hips, urging her to take him deeper in her mouth.

Oral sex had always been something she did to get something in return. Now, with Ben, Ellen realized that feeling his enjoyment, his loss of control was a turn-on for her. She relaxed her throat muscles and gave his pleasure her complete concentration. He was thick, a mouthful in more than one way, but she could handle him. She started moving her head in time with the sharp, short thrusting of his hips. She wished she could reach down and touch herself, bring herself to release at the same time he was getting his.

Again, as if he could read her mind, he stopped her.

"Wait," he said. "I want to taste you. Come up here with me."

Ellen smiled and waited until he had turned on his side, leaving her room to get on the couch with him. Thank God she'd had gotten the extra long, wide sofa. It made for a comfortable bed and was perfect for what she hoped he had in mind.

She lay with her head forward in position to continue to giving him fellatio. He pulled her closer and she could feel the heat of his breath against her mound. He nuzzled his way past her lips and sipped at her creamy essence. She took a deep breath and gave him the same treatment.

She couldn't believe what was happening. Giving oral pleasure at the same time as she was getting it in the sixty-nine position had been an unfilled fantasy over the years. Her husband A.J. had always claimed he couldn't do it because she was too large. She had never trusted him or any of her other lovers since enough to explore the possibilities. But trust wasn't an issue with Ben. Apparently he felt the same way.

Soon though, Ellen couldn't think about anything but the pleasure arrowing through her. It was a double-edged sword of ecstasy, feeling the man of her dreams lapping up every dribble of her cream, while she did the same to him.

Her world became filled with sounds.

His gasps of pleasure and her moans of delight and the creak of leather as they moved together in a horizontal dance of desire blocked out the sound of music still playing in the background.

Her world became filled with smells.

His musk and hers merging together to form an aphrodisiac neither could deny.

Her world became filled with taste.

Sweet and salty, tangy and tart, his body provided a buffet she would remember forever.

Soon, they were both winging their way over the edge. As she milked him dry, she felt him suckle her clit and her orgasm flowed over her in waves.

Exhausted and replete like she'd never been before in her life, Ellen fell in a light daze, her face buried against his now-flaccid cock.

*   *   *

Ben lay on the couch, his arms wrapped around Ellen's hips. This night had eclipsed even his most erotic dreams and it wasn't over.

God, he'd lost count of the number of times he'd come. That hadn't happened since he'd been a randy young recruit.

Even his wildest dreams hadn't prepared him for Ellen. His hands tightened around her hips, moving lower to squeeze her butt. She filled his hands and he had a waking erotic fantasy of turning her over and plunging into her from behind.

He felt himself getting hard. *Again? How was it possible?* He was a healthy man and hadn't had to resort to those little blue pills some men his age had. But there were limits. Too bad his penis didn't know that.

She murmured in her sleep, her breath brushing his skin. Damn, he didn't want this to just be an oral journey, as exciting as that had been. The next time, he was damn well going to be inside her, looking into her marvelous eyes when they came.

So he just had to get her up to speed. And at the rate his erection was growing, it was going to have to be a sprint.

*   *   *

Ellen woke as soon as she felt his cock growing against her cheek. God, how had she gotten so lucky? She was coming up on fifty. Most men her age would have been out for the count by now and she would be left with digging out Mr. Lucky, this month's special toy on sale at BBW. Instead, she had Mr. Lucky in the flesh and she was thanking her Maker.

Feeling her good humor rise, along with her satisfaction level, she lifted up on one elbow and looked up at him.

"Are you glad to see me or is that your weapon, Marine?" She tried for a cross between Lauren Bacall and Madonna.

His chuckle rumbled through him and warmed Ellen from the inside out. Was there anything more attractive than a man so comfortable he could laugh at himself?

"We Marines are taught to take very good care of our weapons," he said. "And my weapon is in desperate need to be fired."

As he spoke, he pulled her up and around so she was face to face with him. He also moved them so he was lying on his back and she was one top of him.

"Oh, I thought maybe you'd fired all your ammunition earlier." She moved, placing her hands on his chest and levering up so she was on her knees, straddling his hips. The muscles of his chest were awesome and, for a moment, she felt like a cat with a nice kneading toy as she curled her fingers into the muscles and curves of his pecs.

But she wouldn't be sidetracked. She straightened her back and moved a bit lower. The action caused her pussy to line up exactly with his cock. Since she was still aroused from his earlier attention and since his weapon seemed to be at the ready again, their skin slipped and slid with gratifying results.

He lay still for a moment, then thrust once. It was a sharp, short thrust of his pelvis and she clenched her thighs tighter around his hips and enjoyed the ride. Thinking she was getting the better of it, she was surprised when his hands moved back down from around her waist to her butt. He spread her checks apart and the action opened her vagina wider, allowing his cock to slide another inch deeper inside her. "Ohhh," she moaned.

"Yesss," he replied.

When she could think coherently, she teased, "We were talking about your ammunition?"

"Ah, yes," he replied after a moment, while they grappled a bit for purchase on the leather sofa. She rocked, he rolled. The result was he slid a couple more hard inches inside her. She felt a bit like the cat who swallowed the canary. He might be controlling this ride, but she was getting most of the pleasure since his wide sex was stretching and filling her to perfection.

"I was going to tell you that Marines never run out of ammunition."

The last syllable of ammunition came out on a moan as Ellen shifted again, bringing her breasts closer to his chest. That movement changed the angle and caused his shaft to rub against her swollen clit. They both groaned at the exquisite feelings racing through them. Her inner muscles were clenching and releasing in time with each move he made. She could feel his cock twitching and swelling and thrilled at the pleasure arcing between them.

"Well, Marine, if ammo isn't the problem, I'm going to say, 'fire at will,'" she whispered bringing her lips down to kiss him.

He didn't need any further instructions as he took them both on a ride like none she'd ever experienced before.

CHAPTER 3

When Ellen awoke, morning was breaking and the sun was angling into her bedroom window, where they'd moved late last night. She stretched and felt deliciously used and well loved.

She turned and looked at the man lying sprawled on his stomach beside her. The night had been more than she'd ever imagined. Now it was time for the morning after. She told herself she had no reason to feel uncomfortable. But there were some misgivings riding to the front.

"I'm getting a heavy feeling over here," he said, opening his eyes and turning on his side so he faced her.

"Sorry," she said. "I'm just hoping you don't have any regrets?"

If he did, she wanted to deal with them now. Even if it meant he never wanted to see her again.

"Why would I have regrets?" he rumbled.

"Well, you probably weren't expecting to come to a party for two and get seduced."

He chuckled. Ellen hoped it wasn't at her.

"No, definitely not."

"Oh. Well, I'd apologize but…"

"But why should you when I enjoyed every enticing minute?" he finished.

"I thought so but…" Ellen chewed on her bottom lip. The next part was harder to say than she'd imagined. Even if it was true. Still, since her divorce, Ellen had made a point of putting all her cards on the table. She wasn't going to stop now, even if it meant losing the man she'd been dreaming about since she was a little girl. "Some men don't like it when a woman makes all the moves."

"Some men are idiots." He reached out to cup her chin in his hand, raising her head so her eyes were looking straight into his.

What she saw there gave her a little thrill. There were honesty, clarity and, incredibly, desire in there. She knew all those were reflected in her eyes as well.

"I've never been an idiot."

Ellen smiled. "I didn't think so, but a gal can never be too sure."

He grinned and the warmth of it moving across his wonderful lips and into his eyes as he ran his gaze over her face thrilled her anew.

"Besides I figured this was about teamwork, like any good Marine action."

He pulled her flush against his body and she felt the way his cock pressed against her pussy. He was hard again and her body, having been schooled well the night before in the pleasure his would bring, began thrumming with desire. Her outer lips swelled and parted as if they were a flower opening to the sun. Her clit began to throb in anticipation and she could feel her juices beginning their trek from her womb. God, he was like a drug and she was an addict after only a few tastes.

When he slid into her, deep, hard and to the hilt, her gasp was quick and delectable.

"Teamwork," he said, his breath stuttering. "You seduce, I seduce. Last night was your party for two. Today we begin my life with you."

Ellen stilled. "Life?"

He smiled and brushed a soft, tender kiss across her lips. "That's right. I let you get away once. It won't happen again."

Ellen held her breath, not really believing what she was hearing. "But what about—"

"There are no 'what abouts,'" he countered. "You're free. I'm free. You're self-employed. I've got my pension from the Marines and I'm going to write novels so I'm self-employed as well. I've got a house, you've got a house. Seems to me like we merge everything and we've got the perfect life."

"But..." Ellen stammered.

"But nothing. This party for two is going to be a life-long affair. Why do you think I came back to Tonawanda? I could've stayed in warm Carolina. I came back for you. I came back to finish what we started when we were five."

"Oh, my," Ellen said. "All this time? You too?"

He frowned. "I'm not going to lie to you. I loved my wife. We made two wonderful kids. But after her death, I knew I wanted to come back here and find you. I knew we'd never given us a chance. We deserve that chance."

"I didn't think you thought of me that way," she said.

"Oh, yeah. But life happened. I came back after my first tour in the Corps, you know right after Grenada, and I was going to ask you to marry me."

"Oh, but that was 1981," she said.

"Right. Your parents said you'd moved to Syracuse and were engaged. I figured I'd waited too long."

"Oh, Ben," Ellen said, "you should've called."

"And what? Tell you to dump your fiancé for some guy you hadn't seen or heard from in five years?"

Ellen started to reply and stopped. He was right. She'd been so enthralled with A.J. then that it wouldn't have mattered.

"And I'm not going to lie to you, Ellen. My life with Belinda was a good one. We weren't passionately in love, but I cared deeply about her. She was a devoted, loving woman. And she gave me the kids. She gave me a chance to find peace inside myself."

Ellen nodded. "I'm glad for you. Even if I can't say the same about my marriage, I can see you're right about changing the past. We can't."

"No, but this isn't about the past. This is about the future," he said. "How about it? You ready to take a chance on an ex-Marine who may be a complete bomb writing sexy thrillers?"

Ellen thought. It was a gamble, but she knew it was right.

"It depends. You ready to take a chance on a big, beautiful woman who runs an eclectic lingerie and sex shop for women?"

He smiled and kissed her deeply, still nestled inside her, the tip of his cock touching the mouth of womb. She felt him throbbing and his cock growing.

"Only if I'm the only one you invite to these parties for two from now on," he said.

"Oh, I can guarantee the invitation will always be open to you." She hugged him close, answering each thrust with one of her own.

As the sun rose high in the sky, they lay together, making love and planning their future.

TRIXIE STILLETTO

"Life is a smorgasbord of men. I believe in diving in like a starving woman hitting an all-you-can-eat buffet!

"Seriously, I love men and have been fortunate enough to work, and play (thank God) with some of the most intriguing ones on this fair earth. There's a little piece of each one in every hero I create. I've had all manner of odd jobs, such as waitress, cook and bottle washer for an all-night dive, truck driver, and, of course, writer. I write erotic romances because it's much more fun to keep the bedroom door wide open.

"My philosophy in life is simple. Love what you do and who you're with and they'll love you in return. Come and join me as I dive into the next delicious dessert."